For a moment, her breath caught.

She found Maddox in her kitchen, scrambling eggs on the stove with a mug of coffee in his hand. The big, tough-looking cowboy seemed at ease in the kitchen, but his jaw was still set in that firm line, and when he looked up at her, a dark wariness had settled in his eyes.

He poured her a cup of coffee and handed it to her, their fingers brushing. A tingle rippled through her at the heat, but he yanked his hand back quickly, then scooped the eggs onto a plate.

"We need to talk."

Rose's instincts surged to life, and she sank into the kitchen chair. She sipped her coffee. "You found something?"

He shook his head then joined her at the table, his big hands wrapped around the mug. "That's just it, Rose. I ran a background check on Thad Thoreau and didn't find anything."

She frowned. "Nothing incriminating?"

"I mean *nothing*," he said, emphasizing the last word. "As in the Thad Thoreau you knew doesn't exist."

LOCK, STOCK AND McCULLEN

USA TODAY Bestselling Author

RITA HERRON

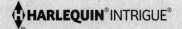
HARLEQUIN® INTRIGUE®

Recycling programs
for this product may
not exist in your area.

ISBN-13: 978-0-373-69850-9

Lock, Stock and McCullen

Copyright © 2015 by Rita B. Herron

Printed in U.S.A.

Rita Herron, a *USA TODAY* bestselling author, wrote her first book when she was twelve, but didn't think real people grew up to be writers. Now she writes so she doesn't have to get a real job. A former kindergarten teacher and workshop leader, she traded storytelling to kids for writing romance, and now she writes romantic comedies and romantic suspense. Rita lives in Georgia with her family. She loves to hear from readers, so please write her at PO Box 921225, Norcross, GA 30092-1225, or visit her website, ritaherron.com.

Books by Rita Herron

The Heroes of Horseshoe Creek

Lock, Stock and McCullen

Bucking Bronc Lodge

Certified Cowboy
Cowboy in the Extreme
Cowboy to the Max
Cowboy Cop
Native Cowboy
Ultimate Cowboy

Harlequin Intrigue

Cold Case at Camden Crossing
Cold Case at Carlton's Canyon
Cold Case at Cobra Creek
Cold Case in Cherokee Crossing

Visit the Author Profile page at Harlequin.com for more titles.

CAST OF CHARACTERS

Sheriff Maddox McCullen—He will put his life on the line to protect the town—especially Rose Worthington. But no one steals Maddox's heart.

Rose Worthington—She thought she was getting married, then her fiancé tried to kill her.

Thad Thoreau—He promised Rose a wedding, but he planned to bury her in the wilderness instead.

Syd and Ramona Worthington—Rose's parents end up dead. Was everything they told her a lie?

Lloyd and Millie Curtain—Did they kidnap Rose as a child?

Donna and Keith Hudgens—Who killed them twenty years ago?

Trina Fields—Rose's friend and assistant at the antiques shop; was she working with Thad to kill Rose?

US Marshal Norton—He's been investigating the disappearance of Hailey Hudgens. But what he finds could get him killed.

Carl Redding—He's not who he says he is.

Bill Redding—He knows the truth about what happened to Rose and her family years ago. Will he kill her to protect his secrets?

Prologue

There were days and nights when he didn't know if he could do it.

Kill Rose.

He remembered her smiling face as a child. That striking red hair. Her singsongy voice. The way she'd looked at him as if he hung the moon.

After she'd disappeared from his life, he'd dreamed about her. Had wanted to find her. Had asked his father over and over where she'd gone and if she was coming back.

His father had told him to forget her.

Then, years later, he'd stumbled onto the truth.

And he hadn't known what to do.

Mistakes had been made, his father said—mistakes that had cost lives.

Mistakes that, in the end, could save others.

His resolve kicked in. Unfortunately there was no turning back now.

Rose Worthington had to die.

Chapter One

Sheriff Maddox McCullen did not want his father to die.

But he was dying anyway, and Maddox couldn't do a damn thing to stop it.

He clenched the doorknob to his father's bedroom door, his stomach fisted into a cold hard knot.

He'd looked up to Joe McCullen his whole life, admired his father's love of the land and the way he'd run the family ranch, Horseshoe Creek. It had been passed down from one McCullen to the next for generations and had made men out of all of them.

His father was as tough as steel and had worked hard. He'd bred thoroughbreds and raised cattle and treated his ranch hands with respect and authority.

But he would be gone soon, and Maddox had to take over. Not that he wasn't prepared. The ranch was in his blood. Taking care of it and the town gave him a purpose.

Mama Mary, the housekeeper and cook who'd practically raised him, met him at his father's door. Short, plump and sturdy, she'd squished him in her big loving arms since he was a child.

"How is he?"

"Resting," she said, her hands gripping a tray holding a teapot and empty cup. "But he wants to see you."

Maddox rapped gently on the door, then pushed it open,

forcing himself not to react to the changes in the big, strong man who'd taught him how to shoot a rifle, ride a horse and rope a calf. His father had lost more weight, his eyes looked sunken and his hand shook as he raised it to cover a cough.

Dammit. Maddox was a take-charge man, a doer. He fixed people's problems. He didn't like this feeling of being helpless.

But his father needed him to be strong. He sure as hell didn't need to see his oldest son break down.

"Dad?"

"Come on in, Maddox. We need to talk."

God, not another discussion of his will and how and where he wanted to be buried.

"What is it? Can I get you something?"

A sheen of sweat coated his father's pale forehead. "No, but there is something you can do for me."

His dad waved him over, and Maddox crossed the room, his boots pounding the wood floor. He dragged the straight chair in the corner next to the bed, straddled it, then removed his Stetson.

"Anything, Dad. You name it."

His father pushed himself to a sitting position, then raked what little hair he had left back from his forehead. "It won't be long now—"

"Don't say that, Dad."

His father's hand shot up to cut him off. "Let me finish. It won't be long, but before I die, I need to see your brothers. There's something I have to talk to each of you about." He coughed again, then struggled for a breath, making Maddox's own chest ache.

"I know you all don't get along," his dad continued, "and that's partly my fault, but it's important I see Brett and Ray."

Maddox swallowed to temper his anger. How could he deny his father's last request? He had a right to say goodbye to each of his sons.

But resentment made him seethe inside. Brett, two years younger than him, had always been irresponsible, a love-'em-and-leave-'em womanizer who'd left home seven years ago chasing his dreams of fame on the rodeo circuit.

And Ray...hell, Ray was the rebellious son. Ever since he turned thirteen, he'd clashed with their father. Maddox had no idea what Ray was up to now, although his youngest brother had skirted the law a few times.

Neither Brett nor Ray had been home to see his father since...well, he couldn't remember when.

That had suited Maddox just fine.

"Will you call them, son?"

Maddox gave a clipped nod.

A weak smile tilted the corner of his dad's mouth. "Families need to stick together. Try to bridge the gap between you and your brothers, son. You all need each other."

Maddox gritted his teeth. He might just be asking the impossible.

"Maddox?"

Words hung in his throat, but he forced them out. "All right, I'll try."

Relief softened the harsh planes of his father's face, and Joe visibly relaxed and closed his eyes. "Just let me know when they get here."

"I will." Maddox strode to the door, but his father's request haunted him.

He would track down Brett and Ray—at least they owed his father the courtesy of a goodbye.

But he didn't expect them to stay. And he didn't need them. He didn't need anyone.

Hell, he'd assure them they could go their separate ways as soon as they paid their visit.

ROSE WORTHINGTON HAD been alone for so long that she couldn't believe she was finally getting married.

She inhaled the lavender scent of the bubble bath, laid her head back and soaked in the decadent claw-foot tub.

Her fiancé, Thad Thoreau, was on the other side of the door putting together a romantic midnight picnic for the two of them to eat in bed. Since neither of them had family to speak of, they'd opted to save money and elope. Pistol Whip, Wyoming, was small-town, a blip on the radar of Wyoming, and was reminiscent of an old Western movie set—not exactly the setting Rose had envisioned for her nuptials.

So they were on their way to Cheyenne for the ceremony. But Thad had pulled off the highway and driven to a cabin off the beaten path, saying they'd have a romantic night before the wedding.

She opened her eyes and glanced at the vintage ivory dress she'd bought for the special occasion tomorrow, her heart fluttering with excitement. The string of pearls Thad had given her lay in the velvet box beside the pearl comb she'd bought for her hair.

She held her hand up and splayed her fingers, admiring the way her French-cut halo diamond sparkled in the candlelight.

Tomorrow she would become Mrs. Thad Thoreau.

Not only would she have a husband to hold her and love her every night, but one day they'd also have a family.

A pang of regret nagged at her for not calling her parents and telling them about her engagement. But they hadn't gotten along since she was a teenager. For some odd reason, ever since she was little, she'd sensed she didn't belong with them. That they were a wrong fit. That she was a problem they didn't know how to get rid of.

And then there had been the awkward conversations she'd overheard, the whispered comments, the *looks*…

The secrets.

They'd wanted to send her away. She'd heard them plotting that one night.

So as soon as she'd turned eighteen, she'd packed and left. Her parents hadn't stopped her. In fact, they'd said it was probably for the best.

Who thought it was best not to talk to your own child?

When she had a baby, she'd make sure her little one knew he or she was loved, that she'd do anything for her child.

The water turned chilly, and she climbed out and dried off, then pulled on her robe. Footsteps sounded from the master bedroom, and she eased open the door.

Thad's voice echoed from where he stood by the window, and she realized he was on the phone.

"Yes, she's the one. I'm positive."

Her heart swelled with gratitude to have found Thad. For so long she'd built walls and kept herself from loving anyone, too afraid to get hurt. But then Thad had walked into her antiques store, Vintage Treasures, and stolen her heart.

Just last week he'd shown her a photograph of the estate he owned in Cheyenne. They were headed there the day after their wedding. Apparently he had inherited family money, which he'd invested, and he'd accumulated his own fortune.

Not that she cared about the money. She wanted companionship, love, a real family...

She started to slip into the room, to inch up behind him and surprise him with a kiss, but he lifted a flyer of a picture of a little girl on a milk carton, a child of about five years old.

"Yes, I'm certain it's her," Thad said. "The woman I'm with is the little girl on the milk carton."

Rose frowned. What was he talking about? How could she be the child? Those ads were placed for missing children…

Thad walked over to the side table, opened his briefcase and removed a pistol. Rose tensed, her heart tripping into double time. Why did he have a gun?

"Don't worry," Thad said, his voice low, as he loaded the weapon. "Your problems will soon be over. She'll be dead by morning."

MADDOX MUTTERED A CURSE as his brother's voice mail clicked on. The first time he'd called, he'd gotten Brett's publicist, but he refused to go through a third party with such a personal matter, so he'd dialed the number again.

Did Brett even answer his own calls?

"Brett, it's me, Maddox. I know we haven't talked in a while—" *two years to be exact*, but he bit back a snide comment "—but it's important. Dad is sick, really sick… He's dying, Brett, and he needs to see you. Call me."

Maddox paced to the fireplace, his gaze drawn to the photograph of him and his brothers when they were young. He was about ten, Brett eight, Ray six. Close in age, they'd wrestled and fought and raced on horseback as kids.

But they'd grown apart after their mother's death and were as different as night and day.

What the hell would he say to them if they did return?

Upstairs, the house seemed quiet and he hoped his father was resting. But his request nagged at Maddox. He didn't especially want his brothers here. He and his father got along great.

He had no idea how he'd live without him.

But…he had to honor his dying request, so he searched for Ray's number. It took him a half dozen calls through various sources he'd had over the past years to track down his youngest brother's current location.

While he punched in Ray's number, he strode to the

bar in the den and poured himself a whiskey. Brett had been irresponsible and wild, but he hadn't possessed Ray's anger and temper.

The phone rang and rang. No answer. *Dammit.*

He left Ray a voice mail, then carried his drink outside to the front porch. The night air filled his lungs, the heat nearly oppressive as he sank onto the porch swing and looked out at the McCullen land. Acres and acres of farm and ranch land that bordered on the mountains and held elk, deer, antelope and other wildlife.

He loved Horseshoe Creek and would keep it up when his father was gone.

But what would he do if Brett or Ray actually wanted to stay and help run it?

COLD FEAR WASHED over Rose. Had she misunderstood Thad?

Had he really said she'd be dead by morning?

"Trust me, no one will find her body."

Rose struggled against the urge to scream. Why would Thad or the person on the other end of the line want her dead?

Was that the reason he'd insisted on them eloping? So he could dump her body in the miles and miles of wilderness around Pistol Whip?

Terror seized her, and she stumbled backward. She caught herself by grabbing the counter, but her hand hit the hair dryer and knocked it to the floor. Suddenly footsteps clattered, and Thad stood in the doorway with the gun in his hand.

The cold look of a seasoned killer greeted her. "Eavesdropping, Rose?"

She shook her head in denial, then glanced around for a weapon, but the bathroom held nothing. Except for her hairspray.

Desperate, she reached for it, but Thad pounced toward her. She jerked up the can and sprayed it at his face. Thad cursed and rubbed at his eyes, then tried to grab her. "You won't get away, Rose."

Taking advantage of the moment, she shoved him and ran. He bellowed and chased after her, waving the gun at her.

A bullet pinged off the wall beside her. Hands shaking, she grabbed her purse and fumbled for Thad's keys on the table.

Suddenly Thad yanked her by the hair and dragged her toward him. She screamed again, fighting him as he threw her to the floor. Her head hit the tile and pain ricocheted through her temple.

He straddled her, then lifted the gun and pointed it at her head.

Rose's vision blurred, death whispering her name. Another image came out of nowhere—another gun. Another man. The sound of a gunshot firing.

Blood spraying everywhere. The floor, the walls…

What was happening…?

Thad's fingers closed around her wrists, tightening so painfully that a sob escaped her.

But reality surfaced and the blurred image of the other shooting faded. The will to live kicked in, giving her a surge of adrenaline, and she used one hand to knock the gun upward. He cursed, and she slammed her fist into his crotch, causing him to double over and roll off her.

She lunged to get away, crawling on her hands and knees into the bedroom, but another gunshot pinged off the floor beside her. Her foot hit the lamp as she tried to get up, sending it crashing to the floor.

Terrified, she reached for the gun and managed to snag it. They struggled with it, both trying to gain control, but the gun went off. Thad grunted, then his eyes widened in shock and he looked down at his chest.

Blood oozed from his torso and soaked his shirt. Frantic, she pushed herself up, grabbed her purse and ran outside. The night sky was dark, void of stars, the endless sea of wilderness swallowing her as she raced to his sedan.

"You can't get away," Thad shouted as he staggered onto the porch after her.

She jumped in the car, keeping her eyes on Thad, her hand trembling as she fumbled with the keys. Three tries and finally the engine fired up.

Thad staggered down the steps, one hand to his bloody chest as he collapsed. She pressed the gas pedal, shifted into Reverse and sped backward, slinging dust in her wake. Thad managed to lift his head and raised the gun and fired again, but he was too far away and the bullet hit the dirt.

She swung the sedan around, stomped on the accelerator and roared down the graveled road to the highway. Nausea clogged her throat as she dug in her purse for her cell phone. *Dammit, she had no service!*

Tears streamed down her face as she drove back toward Pistol Whip. She repeatedly checked over her shoulder in case Thad found a way to follow her. But she didn't stop until she drove into the small town and parked at her rental house.

Fighting a sob, she careened into the drive, threw the car into park and dove out. She ran up the steps to the porch, the keys jangling as she let herself inside. Her phone was ringing as she entered. She flipped on a light in the hallway, then raced to get it.

Whoever it was, she'd get rid of them and call the sheriff. Maddox McCullen would know what to do. He'd help her.

But a sinister voice echoed from the other side of the phone. "You can run, but you can't hide, Rose. I'll find you."

Chapter Two

"No, Ray, I'm not exaggerating." Maddox grimaced at the fact that Ray had even suggested such a thing. "Dad is... dying. Emphysema."

Silence stretched between them for a long minute. Maddox braced himself for Ray to deny his father's request. How he'd explain that to his father he didn't know.

"I'll think about it," Ray said in a belligerent tone.

"Do more than think," Maddox said tersely. "The least you can do is to say goodbye to him. You two might have butted heads, but he is your father."

Ray muttered something ugly that Maddox couldn't understand, but he refrained from asking him to repeat it. He didn't want to know.

He'd given up understanding Ray a long time ago.

His phone beeped that he had another call, and he sighed in relief. *Sad that he welcomed a work call to save him from talking to his own flesh and blood.* "I've got another call I have to take. Now get your butt home. If you don't, I'll track you down and drag you back to Pistol Whip myself."

He didn't bother to wait on a response. He clicked over to answer the other line. "Sheriff McCullen."

"Sheriff, it's Rose Worthington."

Maddox frowned at the way her voice warbled. "What's wrong, Rose?"

"Someone…my fiancé…he tried to kill me tonight."

Shock bolted through Maddox. He'd seen Rose around town, even lusted after her a few times. How could a man not? She had silky red hair, raspberry-ripe lips and a body that made a man want to bury himself inside her.

But he'd been too busy taking care of his father and the ranch, and protecting the town, to get entangled with her. Besides, she'd had a ring on her finger.

"Did you hear me?" Rose said. "He tried to kill me tonight."

Maddox swung into professional mode. "Where are you?"

"My house," Rose said. "Please hurry. I'm afraid he'll come after me."

"What's your address?"

"Two-thirty-one First Street."

"I'm on my way. Just stay on the line." Maddox fastened his holster and gun and hurried outside to his squad car. "Tell me what happened?"

"Before he attacked me, I heard him talking on the phone. He said I'd be dead before morning. He had a gun and I tried to run, and he grabbed me and…the gun went off."

"Are you hurt?" Maddox flipped on his siren and sped toward the street where Rose lived. A Mustang pulled out in front of him, and he beeped his horn and passed it, irritated to see the driver on his cell phone. If he'd had time, he'd have pulled the jerk over, but Rose sounded terrified and he needed to hurry.

She might still be in danger.

ROSE SHIVERED AS she peered out her front window. Was Thad dead?

Or if he'd survived, had he followed her here? Was the person he'd been talking to watching her?

Nausea rolled through her, and she checked to make sure the door was locked, then looked down and realized she was still wearing her robe. Her diamond glittered beneath the light, a reminder of how excited she'd been when she and Thad had left for their trip. All her hopes and dreams were going to come true. Thad loved her.

All lies.

Revulsion mingled with humiliation. She ripped off the ring and tossed it into a drawer, then turned to go upstairs to get dressed. But a noise sounded above and she froze, terrified someone was upstairs.

No…she was probably just paranoid. It was just the furnace…

But…what if the mysterious voice had been calling from inside the house?

A siren wailed, and she pulled back the curtain again and watched as the sheriff's car spun into the driveway. She ran to the door, threw the lock open and rushed outside to the porch.

Seconds later, Sheriff McCullen stepped from the vehicle, his tall frame emerging in the shadows.

"Rose?"

"I'm here." Her voice faded as she ran down the steps toward him. He rushed toward her and she fell into his arms, trembling as a sob escaped her.

MADDOX PULLED ROSE into his arms, cradling her close as she shuddered against him.

He murmured soothing words to her and stroked her hair, hating himself for noticing that it was just as soft as he'd imagined when he'd seen her around town.

What kind of man lusted after a woman when she was quaking in his arms from nearly being killed?

"You're all right, now," he said, lowering his voice to a gentle pitch. Both his brothers had told him that he sounded like a bear when he talked. He couldn't help that he'd been given a deep baritone voice.

It came in handy when he wanted to intimidate a suspect. Not so much when a frightened woman was looking for someone gentle to comfort her.

She clung to him, rasping for breath. "You're safe now, Rose. I won't let anyone hurt you."

She heaved another breath and sniffled, her damp tears soaking his shirt. "I'm sorry. I…didn't know what to do. Who to call."

"I'm the sheriff," he murmured. "I'm here to protect you and everyone in this town."

She nodded against his chest, her sobs finally subsiding. Then she lifted her chin and looked up at him. The pain in her eyes tore at him.

She blinked, tears glistening on her eyelashes in the moonlight that seeped through the clouds.

"Let's go inside and you can tell me everything."

Her lower lip quivered as she released him and folded her arms around her waist. She stumbled on a fallen tree limb on the ground, and he steadied her as they walked up the steps to the porch. When they made it to the doorway, she froze, her eyes widening again in fear.

"I thought I heard a noise upstairs earlier."

He immediately drew his gun and coaxed her aside. "Wait here. Let me check the house."

She nodded and gripped the doorjamb as he scanned the living room to the left. It was clear, so he veered to the right and scanned the kitchen, which was connected to the living room by a breakfast bar. The kitchen was empty, so he took the staircase, his senses honed for sounds of an intruder.

The furnace kicked on, rattling in the silence, and he paused at the top of the staircase to glance into the room to the right.

An iron bed covered in a pale blue-and-white quilt

dominated the room, and an antique dresser held perfume bottles and candles by the bathroom door. He went inside, instincts alert, but saw nothing amiss. A quick check in the closet told him this was Rose's room. Feminine dresses, blouses and shoes filled the closet.

Exhaling slowly, he turned and crossed to the room on the opposite side of the hall. This must be a guest room. The bedding was simple, with a white coverlet on a four-poster Shaker-style bed, and there was a Shaker-style dresser by the wall. The closet held a few containers stacked with extra clothing and items.

But the rooms were clear.

Relieved, he headed back down the stairs. Rose was pacing by the fireplace, her hands worrying the belt of her robe, her face pale.

"No one is upstairs."

"Let me put some clothes on," she said as if she suddenly realized how naked she was.

He nodded. He needed her clothed so he could forget about how she'd felt in his arms and focus on the reason someone had tried to kill her.

Rose threw on a pair of jeans and a T-shirt, fighting a sob. Thad had not only made a fool out of her but he also wanted her dead.

Why?

She glanced in the mirror, shocked at the woman she saw looking back. Her eyes were puffy and red with dark circles beneath them, her face bruised, her hair stringy and tangled. She didn't even look like herself.

Forcing herself to take a deep breath, she dragged a brush through the tangles, then slowly descended the steps, relieved that the sheriff had made it to her house so quickly. She didn't know Maddox McCullen very well, but everyone in town said he was decent and hardworking—a family man.

A man to trust.

God knows she'd trusted the wrong man so far.

"I'll make coffee," she said, desperate for something to do with her hands as she met him at the foot of the staircase.

He gave a grim nod and followed her to the kitchen. An awkwardness, thick and unsettling, cloaked the room as she measured the grounds and filled the coffeepot with water, and they waited on it to brew.

She removed two mugs from the cabinet. "Sugar or cream?"

"Black," he said.

Just as she'd expect from a man like him. Everything about Maddox screamed *alpha male*. Strong, take-charge… masculine.

When it was ready, she filled his mug. He blew on his coffee for a moment, and she gestured toward the pine table and sank into a straight chair. He joined her, still silent, as if he knew she needed time to pull herself together.

Finally she shoved her hair from her eyes, took a deep breath and began. "Thad suggested we elope yesterday," Rose said. "Since neither of us have family that we're close to, I agreed."

"You were anxious to get married?"

She nodded, although heat flooded her cheeks. Why did men make it sound as if women were desperate to get married? "I thought he loved me, that we were going to build a life together."

His jaw tightened. "Go on."

"We decided to go to Cheyenne for the ceremony, but on the way Thad said he knew this private little place off the path, that we could spend the night and have a romantic evening before the wedding."

"So you went to this cabin?"

"Yes." Rose sipped her coffee, tidbits of the last twenty-four hours taunting her. Little things that at the time had seemed insignificant, or even thoughtful, now took on a sinister meaning.

"At first, I thought it was eerie when he drove down this dirt road to the cabin, but he had flowers and wine and... he said he wanted us to be alone, and he made it seem romantic."

"Did you tell anyone where you were going? That you were eloping?"

She shook her head. "I wanted to call Trina, my assistant at the antiques shop, but he said it was more fun if it was our secret, so I texted her that I was taking a couple of days off and asked her to manage Vintage Treasures."

"You didn't tell her where you were going?"

"No, no one knew." Self-disgust ate at her. "Now I understand the reason. He planned to kill me and leave me in the wilderness so no one would find me."

Silence lingered for a full minute before Maddox asked, "What happened at the cabin?"

She massaged the scar at the base of her temple, a nervous habit she'd had since she was young. "I went to take a bubble bath while he was supposedly setting up a picnic for us. But when I got out of the tub, I heard him talking on his cell phone."

"Who was he talking to?"

"I don't know." The conversation echoed in her head, making her blood run cold. "I heard him say that I was the one... At first, I thought he meant it romantically. That I was the one he loved, the one he was meant to be with."

The irony of that statement seemed to hit both of them. "Then what happened?"

"He held up this flyer. It had a picture of a little girl on a milk carton on it."

Maddox's brows drew together in a deep frown. "A little girl?"

"She was about five years old." She fidgeted, still trying to make sense of it. "Then he said I was the one they'd been looking for, and that I'd be dead by morning."

A heartbeat passed. "He meant that you were the girl on the milk carton?"

"Yes," Rose whispered, her agitation mounting. "But that doesn't make sense."

"He didn't elaborate?"

"No." She shivered. "Instead, he pulled a gun from his briefcase."

"Did you know he carried a weapon?"

"No, I'd never seen it." She twisted her hands together. "But it scared me, and I stumbled. Then he saw me and came after me." Her breath came out in spurts as fear once again seized her. "He shot at me and missed, and we fought. I tried to get away but the gun went off again."

Maddox covered her hand with his. "Go on."

"I shot him, Maddox. I didn't mean to, but the bullet hit him." She blinked back more tears, her heart pounding. "Blood soaked his shirt, and I was terrified, so I ran to the car. He staggered to the door and fired at me again."

Another tense silence. "Did he follow you?"

"I don't know, he collapsed on the ground," she cried. "I think I might have killed him."

Chapter Three

Tears filled Rose's eyes again, the terror returning. She could still see the sinister look in Thad's eyes, see him lunging for her with that gun.

"You didn't call an ambulance or the police?"

Rose tensed. "No, I tried my cell as I was leaving and there was no service. Then all I could think about was escaping."

He lifted her wrists, a muscle ticking in his jaw as he noted the bruises. "He grabbed you here?"

"Yes," she said, remembering the horror of his fingers clenching her as Maddox gently stroked the tender area.

"Can you tell me where this cabin is?" Maddox said.

"I don't know the name of the road we turned off on. But...I could probably find it."

He stood. "I have to go out there and see if he's still alive."

Nerves fluttered in Rose's stomach. *What if Thad was dead? Would she be arrested for murder?*

MADDOX CONSIDERED CALLING the Cheyenne Police Department, but figured he'd assess the situation first and find out if Thoreau was dead or alive.

He texted Mama Mary to let her know that he might not be home tonight, and to call him if his father's condition changed.

"I understand it may be difficult for you, Rose, but do you mind riding with me and guiding me to the cabin?"

Wariness darkened her eyes, but she squared her shoulders as if to gather her courage. "No, I'll take you there."

He led the way outside, giving her time to lock the door. She still seemed wobbly as they walked to his car, and he opened the passenger door and waited until she settled inside before he circled around to the driver's seat.

Anxiety vibrated between them as he veered onto the highway and drove through Pistol Whip, which was situated in a flat stretch between the mountains. Land spread out before them, miles and miles that were untamed, where antelope, deer, elk and other wildlife thrived.

Tourists wanting a frontier town and trail riding, or a layover on their way to Laramie or Cheyenne, often stopped in Pistol Whip. Hikers, mountain climbers and fishermen especially took advantage of the proximity to the majestic mountains and river.

Locals had created a small museum showcasing the area's history. Apparently in the late 1800s, a famous gunslinger had ridden through the hills in search of a hideout. When three local vigilantes discovered his identity, they strung him up in town and pistol-whipped him to death.

The town council at the time dubbed the town with the name Pistol Whip to remind people that they couldn't take the law into their own hands.

"Tell me about your fiancé," Maddox finally said. Any background information on their relationship would be helpful.

Rose toyed with a string on the bottom of her T-shirt. "We met in Cheyenne," she said. "I was there for an antiques show, and he was on business."

"What kind of business?"

"He worked...works for an energy company."

"Did he mention the name of it?"

Rose rubbed at her temple just as he'd seen her do at her house. Obviously a nervous gesture. As she pushed her hair back, he noticed a scar at her hairline, a jagged one that disappeared into the hair on the crown of her head.

It looked as if it ran deep and went across her skull. He wondered what had happened.

"I don't think he ever said the name of it. Or if he did, I forgot."

Because she'd been snowed by his charm.

"Did he mention anyone he worked with? Business clients or friends?"

Rose chewed her bottom lip for a minute. "No. Wait...I heard him talking to someone named Carl once."

"Do you remember his last name?"

She shook her head. "He just said he'd fax him the information he needed. But I didn't hear what the conversation was about."

Had he been vague because he was hiding something?

"Do you have one of Thad's business cards?"

"I might have one at the house."

"Good. When we go back, get it for me."

Cacti and scrub brush dotted the land as he left the small town and drove through the countryside. Winter had set in, the ground dry and barren-looking.

"How long did you date?"

"About six months." She gave a self-deprecating laugh. "Obviously he had no intention of ever marrying me. He... was probably lying to me the entire time. But why would he kill me over a photo or think I was that girl?"

"Good question." Maddox grimaced. This guy had targeted Rose. "The fact that he was talking to someone on the phone about you means he was either working for this other person or he had an accomplice."

Rose turned to look out the window, her face drawn as if she was lost in the horror of the evening.

"What about his family? You said earlier that you were eloping."

Rose nodded. "He said he lost his parents a few years ago, but he'd inherited family money."

Could have been more lies. Hell, Thoreau might not even be his real name. "What about yours?"

"My parents...well, we haven't spoken in a while." She lapsed into a sullen silence. Obviously the subject was painful for her and she didn't want to elaborate.

He wouldn't probe for now. Not unless he discovered her family had something to do with Thoreau.

But if Thoreau was dead...hell, he'd have to dig into every aspect of her life. Because Rose would need a defense.

If the flyer of that picture on the milk carton was there as she said, that would be a place to start.

ROSE WANTED NOTHING more than to forget what had happened earlier this evening. But she had to find out if Thad was dead.

Fear clenched her stomach at the thought that she'd killed a man, even if it was in self-defense. But she'd never been the kind of woman to run from a problem and live in naive bliss.

Just as she'd faced the fact that her parents hadn't wanted her, that she'd been a mistake. Well, they had taken care of her, but there had always been an awkwardness between them, a distance, as if the woman and man, Ramona and Syd, didn't want to get too close.

As if they couldn't really love her.

She'd been a difficult child, they'd said. Sullen, angry, withdrawn at times...

A crooked tree with several broken branches caught her eye, and recognition dawned. She remembered the tree because it had made her think of herself. She'd felt broken and alone so many times.

"Down that road," she said, her voice rough with emotion.

Maddox swung the car onto the side road. "You're sure?"

She nodded and rubbed at her arms as a chill swept over her. "When Thad veered onto the road, I remember wondering if he'd made a wrong turn. It looked like we were going nowhere. But he promised me a night I'd never forget." A sarcastic laugh rumbled from her. "That's certainly true."

Maddox didn't comment. He didn't need to.

Winning her trust had been part of Thad's charm. He'd intentionally driven off the grid, far away from other houses and people so no one would hear her scream for help when he killed her.

The barren land and ridges of the nearby mountain range sent another chill through her. If he'd succeeded, he would have dumped her body in a ravine or thrown her over a cliff and left her for the animals to ravage.

And no one would have looked for her or even realized she was dead.

MADDOX HOPED TO HELL Rose was telling him the truth. The whole truth and not a fabricated version she'd invented to cover some dark secret.

The idea of locking her in a cell held no appeal. But he was a man of the law and he'd do whatever necessary to see that justice was served.

He made a quick call to his deputy, Roan Whitefeather, and asked him to make the rounds in the town because he was busy, but he didn't explain. He'd check things out himself first.

The car bounced over the ruts in the dirt road, desolate land passing, the sliver of moonlight barely illuminating the trees and landscape. An animal darted into the wooded area to the left, and Rose pointed to a narrow side road.

"There. The cabin is that way."

Night noises surrounded them, the deserted area eerie

with the sound of a coyote howling, a reminder that the state was on an alert for coyotes with rabies. And that it was the perfect place to dispose of a body.

But what motive did Thoreau have? And who else wanted to find Rose?

"The cabin is in that hollow by the creek," Rose said.

Maddox's instincts went on alert as he scanned the area for a car or another person waiting to ambush them.

But there was no car and he didn't see movement. Not even a light on in the cabin nestled in the copse of pines.

"Did you turn the lights off when you left?" Maddox asked.

Rose tensed, straightening to examine the graveled drive as they approached. "No, I was in a hurry, running to get away."

Senses alert, Maddox slowed the car and parked, his gaze fixed on the cabin and dark woods surrounding it. "Did Thoreau say how he found this place?"

"No." Rose rubbed at her arms again as if cold. "I didn't ask. I…I trusted him."

Maddox studied the area for tire marks. With his headlights shining on the ground, he spotted one set that had made indentations into the dirt. Obviously Rose's tire prints as she'd backed away and sped from the cabin.

He cut the engine and his lights, that coyote still howling like it was hunting for prey, and he removed his holster and checked his Colt.

He reached for the door handle. "Wait here and let me check out the house."

"What if the other man is out here?" Rose asked in a strained voice.

"There's no sign of a car here," he pointed out.

Rose touched his hand. "Let me go with you. I…don't want to stay here alone."

Maddox sighed, hating the fear in her voice. But he understood it. She'd been through hell and back tonight.

"All right, but stay behind me."

She nodded, and he grabbed a flashlight, climbed out and shut his door gently, his boots crunching grass and twigs as he walked around to the passenger side. She opened her door and slid out, and he gestured for her to stay close as they walked up to the porch.

The flashlight illuminated the ground, and Maddox scanned it for evidence, also darting suspicious looks around the perimeter of the property and front of the cabin.

"I don't understand," Rose whispered. "He chased me out here and collapsed at the bottom of the porch."

Maddox narrowed his eyes and shone the flashlight across the porch. Rose sounded so sure of what she was saying, so frightened.

But there was no body. No blood.

No sign of Rose's fiancé anywhere.

Chapter Four

Rose stared at the empty porch in shock. "I don't understand. He fell…and he was bleeding." She pointed to the bottom step, where she'd seen Thad collapse, blood oozing from his wound. "I…didn't see him get up."

"But you were trying to escape?"

"Yes." She looked at the drive. "His sedan was under that tree."

"Where did you say he was hit with the bullet?"

Rose lifted her gaze, the images of her struggle with her fiancé flashing back. "The chest…at least I thought that was where the bullet went in, but it happened so fast."

Maddox shined his flashlight all along the boards of the porch floor. "Either he got up on his own or someone helped him." He kneeled and examined the slats. "I don't see blood, either."

"But he *was* bleeding," Rose said, confused. She started inside the house, but Maddox caught her arm.

"Wait and let me search the place first." His dark eyes flickered with worry. "He could be hiding, Rose, nursing his wound."

Maddox held his gun at the ready and gestured for her to stay back. Rose clutched her hands together, trembling as he inched inside the cabin.

Had Thad survived?

If he had...he might come back for her.

MADDOX EASED INTO the entryway, his senses alert as he glanced left and right. He strained to hear sounds from inside—footsteps, breathing—but he heard only the floor creaking and the eerie sound of a faucet dripping in the silence.

He scanned the living area but other than a faded couch and chair, the room was empty. No signs of blood or bullet casings either.

He crept to the adjoining kitchen and looked around. Hadn't Rose mentioned that Thad was planning a picnic?

There was no evidence of food or drink, or that *anyone* had been here. The sink was empty, even clean, and he opened the cabinets to see dishes and glasses neatly organized.

The dripping water pinged again, and he headed toward the sound and found the leak in the tub. The scent of cleaning chemicals and bleach assaulted him.

Had Thad cleaned up?

He still didn't see blood, but he'd get his kit from his car and spray with luminol. That might turn up something. Although it was possible the bullet had only grazed Thad.

Veering to the left of the bathroom, he found the bedroom. An iron bed draped in a quilt sat against the wall with the window, while an antique dresser and full-length mirror were also in the room.

No sign of anyone. No flyer of a missing girl on a milk carton. And no luggage...

If Rose and Thad were traveling, where were their things? Hadn't she brought a suitcase?

If she'd been running for her life, she wouldn't have stopped to get it.

He checked the closet next but found it empty as well.

Either Rose was confused or lying or…her fiancé had survived and escaped and cleaned up any evidence he'd ever been in the cabin.

Another scenario surfaced though—Thad's accomplice could have gotten rid of Thad's body, then cleaned up to cover his own tracks.

She had received a threatening call though. He needed to check her phone to verify that a call had actually come through. *Because…he didn't believe her?*

No, checking her phone records would be standard procedure. And if he could trace the number of the caller, it might lead to the person who wanted to kill her.

ROSE STARTLED AT the sound of the wind rustling leaves, and pivoted to look into the woods. A coyote's howl unnerved her. She'd heard that coyotes had been attacking other animals, killing cats and dogs, and that they carried rabies.

Was the animal close by?

Questions swirled in her brain, making her head throb. *Was Thad? Could he have survived that gunshot wound?*

She backed against the wall and studied the floor again, wondering how anyone could have cleaned up that blood so quickly.

If Thad was alive, where was he?

Maybe the caller—Thad's partner—had been near the cabin and Thad had phoned him after she'd left.

Footsteps pounded then, and Maddox appeared in the doorway. "The house is clear. No indication of Thad or anyone else."

Rose bit down on her lip. "I can't believe this is happening."

"Rose, did you bring a suitcase here?"

Rose nodded. "Yes, and my wedding gown. I was taking a bath right before I heard Thad on the phone."

His eyes darkened as he studied her. "You didn't take any of your things with you?"

"No, I told you that I ran from the house. He knocked me down and we struggled. A lamp broke…"

She elbowed past him and surveyed the living room. No broken lamp. Everything was in its place.

She pointed to the small pine table. "Thad brought a picnic basket filled with goodies—cheese and crackers and fruit and wine. We were going to have a midnight picnic after my bath."

"There's no food or picnic basket here," Maddox pointed out.

Frantic, she yanked open the drawer on the end table, then the small corner desk, searching for the flyer of the picture of the girl on the milk carton, but the drawers were empty. "He had that flyer. He was looking at it."

She rubbed her temple, retracing her steps. "I had a glass of wine with my bath." She rushed over to the kitchen and searched the cabinets. There were four wineglasses, all clean and dry as if they hadn't been used.

She swung open the pantry door to check the garbage can, but it was empty.

"He brought a picnic. I swear he did. He must have thrown everything out."

"I didn't see a garbage bin outside, but I'll look for one." His footsteps pounded on the floor as he headed toward the door.

Confused, she dashed into the bedroom. The quilt was turned up on the bed, pillows placed strategically, the curtains closed—and the room was empty. Her suitcase and the wedding dress she'd hung over the doorway were gone.

Head spinning, she darted into the bathroom. The toiletry bag she'd set on the vanity wasn't there now. The tub looked clean, no signs of the bubble bath she'd taken earlier. Even her wet towel was gone.

She felt Maddox come up behind her, smelled his masculine scent. "I didn't find any garbage outside."

"I had my things in here, too," she said, still in shock. "I took a bubble bath and my cosmetic bag was on the vanity, and my wedding dress was hanging over the door. I could see it from the tub."

"You're sure this is the right cabin?" Maddox asked.

"Did you see another one out here?" She whirled on him, hating the doubt in his voice. *Did he think she was making this up? That she was delusional?*

"I recognize the furniture, the quilt on the bed." She searched for a way to convince him. "There's an extra blanket in the bedroom closet, and…a Bible in the nightstand." She raced to the nightstand, opened it and pulled the Bible out. "See. It's here."

He checked the closet and noted the blanket.

But she realized that proved nothing. Most places had extra blankets in the closet.

"Thad was shot," she said emphatically, determined to assure Maddox—and herself—that she wasn't going crazy. "I saw the blood, and he fell. There's no way he could have cleaned everything out like this."

"I'm going to grab my crime kit from the car," Maddox said. "I'll be right back."

She wrapped her arms around her waist, shivering as images of Thad holding that gun taunted her.

She'd never seen such a cold look in anyone's eyes, such a metamorphosis from charming and loving to…evil. She'd known then that he could kill her and not feel an ounce of remorse.

She just didn't understand the reason.

MADDOX GRITTED HIS TEETH. If Rose was a complete stranger, he might question if she was lying about what had happened tonight.

There wasn't a shred of visible evidence to support her story.

Yet the fear in her eyes, the conviction in her voice, the betrayal he heard in her pained tone—none of it was fake.

But what possible motive would anyone have to kill Rose?

That was a question he would probe later. For now, he had to process this place and see if he could find something to corroborate Rose's story.

Maddox strode out to his car, opened the trunk and retrieved his crime kit. He photographed the exterior of the cabin and the driveway, focusing on the tire marks that indicated another car had been parked there at some point, then photographed the landing at the bottom of the steps where Rose indicated Thoreau had collapsed.

Rose stood on the porch watching him as he climbed the steps. He pulled on latex gloves, and kneeled to spray luminol on the floorboards of the porch. The scent of bleach swirled around him, a sign that someone had recently cleaned.

Which was suspicious in itself. If the place was deserted and no one had been here, why would it smell as if it had just been scrubbed?

At first, the luminol didn't indicate anything, but he continued to spray, visually searching each inch.

He targeted the doorjamb and leaned closer to examine the corner. There—a small drop of blood. It had seeped into a splintered section. Whoever had scrubbed had missed it.

He glanced up at Rose. "There is a speck of blood."

Her relieved sigh echoed in the air. "I told you he was bleeding."

"It isn't much," Maddox said. "But I'm going to check the rest of the house and dust for prints. Also, if he was shot, there should be a bullet casing somewhere."

"Thank you, Maddox."

He shrugged. "I'm just doing my job, Rose." Although protecting her seemed innate to him.

She stepped aside while he went to work. He dusted the doorways, doorknobs, table, kitchen counter and desk. Finally he found a partial on the pantry doorknob. Maybe Thad or his accomplice had left it when they'd grabbed the garbage.

He sprayed more luminol on the floor in the doorway and found a few tiny traces the bleach hadn't erased. Someone had definitely been hurt here.

Which made it more suspicious that there were no fingerprints. Not even Rose's, on the bathtub or the closet door where she claimed she'd hung her wedding gown.

Whoever had cleaned the place knew what they were doing. Maybe Thad was a professional hit man? Or his accomplice was?

But there was no bullet casing. No bullet hole, either. Odd. The bullet must not have been a through and through, meaning it might still be in Thoreau.

When he finished processing the house, he found Rose on the porch again, sitting on the porch swing, her expression tormented as she stared out at the sharp ridges beyond them. "I'll need your prints for comparison purposes."

Rose nodded, her expression so forlorn that he joined her on the swing.

"You don't think I'm crazy or that I made this up?" Rose asked softly.

He laid his hand over hers, unable to keep himself from offering her a token gesture of comfort. "No. I think whoever cleaned up here was a pro. They knew what they were doing. But still, I found a little blood, and a partial print."

Hope flickered in Rose's expression but she rubbed at her temple again as if a headache pulsed behind her eyes. "It's strange, but when I saw Thad's blood, I...saw flashes of blood everywhere. And all you found was a tiny bit."

He didn't know what to say to that.

"We'll get to the bottom of this, Rose." He squeezed her hand, his gut tightening as she looked into his eyes.

He'd do everything in his power to fulfill his promise.

After all, it was his job to protect the citizens in Pistol Whip. And he'd be damned if Thad or this other man would get to Rose again.

IT WAS WELL into the night when Maddox drove Rose home. Fatigue pulled at her, but she was too nervous to think about sleep.

Maddox walked her to her door. "I'll send these samples to the forensic lab tomorrow and see what we get back." He hesitated. "Let me come in and search your house before I leave."

Rose nodded, relieved not to be left alone yet. She unlocked the door, her breath catching when Maddox brushed against her. She'd always thought cowboys were sexy. So why had she fallen for Thad when he was the opposite?

A businessman. Or so he'd said. Then again, every word that had come out of his mouth might have been a lie.

She flipped the light switch in the foyer, and waited while Maddox combed through her small house, searching each room.

His wide jaw was set in stone as he descended the staircase.

"Did you find something?"

He shook his head, and she glanced down at her fingers. The ink smear where he'd taken her prints mocked her with the horror of the night.

"Rose?" Maddox approached, his expression guarded. "I need to have the lab check your phone records to see where that threatening call came from. Is that all right?"

"Of course." Her chest ached as emotions pummeled her. "Do whatever you have to do." She dug through a drawer for a minute, then retrieved a business card and handed it to him. "Here, this is Thad's."

Maddox scanned the card. "Thanks, I'll check into it."

"You think he really worked there or was that a lie, too?"

"I don't know, but I'll find out. I'm going to dust his car for prints, too. It's possible Thoreau wasn't his real name."

He rubbed her arms with his hands. Hands that felt strong but tender. Hands that made her want to lean into him and never let go.

But that was crazy. She'd trusted Thad, and look where that had gotten her.

Maddox was only here to help her find the man—or men—who wanted her dead.

She needed his help as the sheriff, nothing more. And she couldn't forget it.

Chapter Five

Maddox had considered calling the sheriff in Laramie, but without evidence of a body, he'd look like a fool.

Rose sank into the kitchen chair as if she was too exhausted to stand. "What do we do now?"

He joined Rose at the table, his hands splayed on top. "Technically there's no crime to report. Well, except that you were attacked, and I'll document that and your story. But there's no body and the blood is minimal, so it's not enough to warrant calling in any other law enforcement at this time."

"But Thad Thoreau is either dead or missing."

"I realize that," Maddox said. "And I didn't say I wouldn't investigate. But I don't plan to inform other authorities until I do some research myself."

Rose fidgeted but looked relieved. "It was self-defense, Maddox. I swear it was."

He might not believe a stranger, but he believed Rose.

Or was that his libido talking? He'd always been attracted to her, but his daddy had drilled into him not to chase a woman who was already attached to another man.

And Rose had been wearing that big diamond on her finger.

Her heart must have been broken at her fiancé's betrayal.

"I'll check hospitals, ERs, urgent-care facilities and the

morgue in case the person Thoreau was talking to on the phone carried him for medical help."

"You think he had an accomplice? That he cleaned up the blood to cover for Thad's attack on me?"

"It's possible." Another thought occurred to Maddox. "I should search the land and woods surrounding the cabin in case he buried Thoreau there."

Rose shuddered visibly. "I didn't think of that."

Maddox squeezed her hand again. Her fingers felt icy, a tremor running through her. "That's my job, Rose. Why don't you get some rest?"

Rose chewed her bottom lip. "I…I'm not sure I can sleep."

Maddox sucked in a breath, forcing himself not to react physically to the way she folded her fingers into his palm and clung to him. She was suffering from shock and obviously scared to be alone.

Normal for a victim of a crime.

"I'll stay here and make sure you're safe."

Her lips parted in surprise as she angled her face toward him. "I can't ask you to do that, Sheriff."

"Maddox," he said, his voice gruff. "And you didn't ask. I'm the law around here. I wouldn't feel right leaving you unprotected, not until we find out what happened to your fiancé and find the person who made that threatening phone call."

Rose's gaze met his, shock still flaring in her eyes. "I still can't wrap my head around the idea that Thad lied to me all along, that he…wanted me dead."

"That'll take time." He slowly pulled his hand from hers. "By the way, do you have a photograph of Thoreau?"

Rose hesitated a moment, then reached inside her purse for her phone and accessed a selfie of her and the man. "Thad didn't want formal pictures taken, but I managed to snap this one at dinner one night."

Maddox scrutinized the man's face. He looked to be in his midthirties, had an angular face, short brown hair, thick brows, a cleft in his chin and eyes that looked a muddy hazel.

"Will that help?" Rose asked.

"Yes, thanks. Now go to bed. I'm going to make some phone calls and see what I can find out."

Rose pushed herself up from the table with a sigh. "Thank you, Maddox. I…appreciate all you've done tonight."

He stood, tempted to pull her into his arms and comfort her again. But he needed to maintain his distance.

She had been involved in a crime, and he had to remain objective until he learned the truth about what happened earlier.

The cop voice in his head, the one that had been lied to by other suspects, warned him to tread carefully. Two years ago, an alleged victim who'd come running to him for help had actually turned out to be the mastermind of a criminal ring.

Actually he didn't know that much about Rose herself. Only that she'd moved here a few months ago and opened an antiques shop.

It was far-fetched, but it was possible that she'd killed the man and buried him herself, then concocted this story about the attack.

ROSE CLIMBED THE steps to the bedroom, her emotions in a tailspin. Relief that Maddox was in her house calmed her nerves, but the moment she went into the bedroom and saw the music box Thad had given her the night he proposed, tears flooded her eyes.

The fact that he'd remembered her love of music boxes had moved her even more. It was the one special thing she and Ramona Worthington had bonded over. She'd thought that the gift was so romantic, that Thad really loved her, that they'd spend a lifetime together.

She'd had no idea he'd wooed her into trusting him so he could end her life.

She lifted the lid to the music box, once again mesmerized by the sound of the love song and the dove twirling on the top. Something about the antique music box stirred a distant memory, reminded her of a music box she'd seen before, maybe as a child.

But she couldn't place what it looked like or the song it was playing.

An image of a woman's hand teased at her memory, and a soft voice whispered to her that the music box had belonged to her grandmother.

But her mother had never mentioned a grandmother. In fact, when she'd asked about other relatives, her mother had clammed up.

Heart heavy, she stripped, pulled on a gown and brushed her teeth. But the sight of her ashen, tear-streaked face in the mirror reminded her of the horror of her near death.

She splashed cold water on her face, then fell into bed and drew the covers above her, clenching them as the nightmare of the evening played over and over in her head.

She had escaped Thad tonight.

But would he or the man on the phone come back and try to kill her?

MADDOX WAITED UNTIL Rose disappeared up the steps, then strode out to Thad's sedan and searched the car. Nothing inside that looked suspicious. The vehicle was registered to Thad Thoreau.

He retrieved his kit from his car and dusted the interior for prints, then placed the prints in his kit to take to the lab the next morning.

Then he retrieved his computer. He set it up at Rose's

kitchen table, then accessed a list of local hospitals, ERs, urgent-care facilities and morgues. He sent them a picture of Thad for identification purposes.

A few phone calls later, and he'd found nothing. "Call me if this man turns up, or if you get a patient suffering from a gunshot wound." He left his number, and reminded the nurse on the phone that the man he was looking for might be armed and dangerous, to alert security and not confront him.

Technically, doctors were required to report any gunshot wound, but sometimes things slipped between the cracks. Especially if the patient, or the person who brought the patient in, was armed and threatened the health care workers.

The fact that Thoreau hadn't been admitted could mean that his accomplice had carried him somewhere off the grid for medical help.

Or that he was dead.

Another reason to search the property tomorrow.

He accessed the national police databases and ran a search on Thad Thoreau.

First of all, the man's name didn't pop up as having an arrest record. Neither did it appear that he'd served in the military.

In fact, when he plugged Thoreau's name into the DMV database, he found three different Thad Thoreaus but none of them matched the picture Rose had shown him. One Thad Thoreau was ninety and in a nursing home, another was deceased and the third was a professor in Salt Lake City.

He checked each of their backgrounds to see if any one of them had a son named Thad, but hit a dead end.

Frustrated, he spent the next hour researching the company listed on Thad's business card, but couldn't find a company with that name. The company was bogus—part of Thad's cover.

If Thoreau was a professional killer, he'd probably used an alias. He phoned Devon Littleman, the best IT analyst he knew at the lab, and emailed him Thoreau's photograph. "We need to know his real name," Maddox said after he'd explained the situation.

"This might take a while."

"Let me know what you find. I'm dropping off his prints tomorrow." Thoreau could have randomly pulled the identity from a source like a computer or a phone directory, or he could have chosen it from a gravestone or obituary notice.

Whatever his name, Thad Thoreau was not who he claimed to be.

So who was he?

And why had he come after Rose?

It had something to do with the girl on the milk carton...

"Can you put a trace on Rose Worthington's phone in case the man who threatened her calls again?"

"I'm on it."

"Devon, pull it up now. She received a threatening call tonight. I want to know where it came from."

"Hang on."

Maddox drummed his fingers on the table as he waited. Finally Devon came back.

"There was only one call made to her number tonight. Looks like it came from a burner phone. Sorry, but I can't trace it."

Damn. "Thanks. Call me if you find anything else."

Maddox hung up. Curious, he plugged Rose's name into the computer and ran a check on her. Guilt needled him for invading her privacy. But she needed his help, and he couldn't uncover Thoreau's motive for wanting her dead if he didn't know more about her.

The wind picked up outside, rattling the windowpanes and whistling through the house. He glanced at the stairs to make sure Rose wasn't coming back down, but didn't see her or hear footsteps. Hopefully, she'd fallen asleep.

Maybe tomorrow she'd remember more details about her fiancé that would help his investigation.

Rose's name appeared on the DMV database, the photograph taken two years before. She had no arrest record, had lived with parents named Ramona and Syd Worthington before moving to Pistol Whip. Ramona, now in her fifties, worked in a gardening center while Syd worked with a freight company.

He studied the picture of the couple, looking for similarities to Rose, but her features were softer, rounder, her eyes a deep amber instead of Ramona's blue or Syd's brown.

Rose said she and her parents were estranged. What had happened between them?

Not that it was pertinent to the case, but if he wanted to know the reason someone wanted to kill Rose, he had to learn everything he could about her.

And that included tracking down the girl on the milk carton.

How old was Rose now? He checked her birth date on the driver's license photo. Twenty-five.

Which meant that the photograph of the missing child—hadn't she said she was around four or five?—would have been posted about twenty years ago.

Determined to get to the bottom of the mystery, he accessed the database for missing and exploited children and searched for girls who'd disappeared around that time. Hundreds of pictures showed up, enough to make him sweat under the collar.

He entered Rose's name to narrow down the search, and waited, but that yielded nothing.

If he knew the state where the girl disappeared from, it would help.

It was also possible that since the photo had been circulated, she'd been found alive and returned to her family, or she was...dead.

He compared Rose's name with a list of children reported as deceased during that time frame. There were two other girls with the last name Worthington, but one was a teen found dead from an overdose, the other a runaway who'd eventually gone home on her own.

The search led to countless other girls named Rose, and it took him nearly an hour to sort through them and run a comparison.

Dammit, he needed better software to show age progression. Something he'd have to speak to the county about, although he doubted it would do much good. Pistol Whip was such a blip on the Wyoming map that the big cities rated the nicer, more sophisticated equipment.

His eyes were starting to blur from fatigue, so he decided to rest his head for a while. It was already 4:00 a.m.

Tomorrow he had to go back to the cabin and search for a grave.

Weary from the night's events, he closed the laptop. He walked to the window and checked out the front, then to the rear and surveyed the wooded backyard.

Everything seemed quiet. Peaceful.

Rose was safe.

But as he stretched out on her sofa, he laid his gun on his chest just in case Thoreau or his partner returned to kill her in the night.

HANDS TIGHTENED AROUND *Rose's throat. She tried to scream, but she couldn't breathe. Couldn't make a sound come out.*

Terrified she was going to die, she struggled to pry the man's hands from around her neck, but he was so strong she couldn't budge his fingers, and his nails cut into her skin.

Tears streamed down her cheeks as her body began to convulse. Still she kicked and clawed...

Then the hands lifted from her throat, and the cold blunt edge of a gun barrel settled against her temple. "You can run, but you can't hide, Rose. I'll find you."

She struggled to see, but darkness surrounded her. Then the red...so much red...blood everywhere. Splattering the walls and the floors...splattering her. Her knees. Her hands.

Her face...

A scream tore from her throat and she tried to move, but fear paralyzed her.

Then the sound of gunfire exploded into the room. Bullets pinging off the wall. A man's voice. A woman's cry for help.

She closed her eyes and tried to crawl toward her, but the world was fading away into gray...

"Rose?" Another hand gripped her arm, this time firm but gentle. "Rose, it's me, Maddox. Wake up."

She jerked her eyes open at the sound of that familiar voice, but she was trembling so badly that fear immobilized her. She could only look into his eyes and whisper his name.

His gaze connected with hers. He soothed her tearstained face, then pulled her into his arms.

She buried her head against him, hating to be weak, but terrified of what she'd seen in her nightmare. The room where she'd been—she didn't know where it was, except there were antiques there and lace curtains, and music had been playing, a soft lyrical tune like the one in the music box Thad had given her.

Only she hadn't been at the cabin...and it wasn't Thad holding the gun to her head. She'd seen this man's eyes.

They were black, the blackest of black, as if they were hollowed empty holes in his face.

As if they were the devil's eyes.

Was the man a figment of her imagination, the face she'd conjured up to go with the man who'd threatened her on the phone?

And all that blood…it was almost as if she'd been there. Seen someone die.

Someone she'd loved…

But that was impossible. If she'd witnessed a death or murder, she would remember it, wouldn't she?

Chapter Six

Maddox rubbed Rose's shoulders to soothe her. "It's all right, Rose, you're safe now. I won't let him hurt you." He continued to comfort her with soft nonsensical words until she calmed.

"I'm sorry, Maddox," Rose whispered. "It was just a nightmare. Except it seemed so real."

He steeled himself against the way she'd felt against him, all soft womanly curves. It had been a long time since he'd been with a woman. Between his job as sheriff and taking care of his ranch and his father, he was usually too exhausted at night to consider dating.

That had to be the reason he was reacting so strongly every time Rose touched him.

Maddox stood to put some distance between them. "Understandable after last night. Go back to sleep."

She licked her lips. "I don't think I can."

Early morning sunlight streamed through the sheer lacy curtains of her window, dappling her skin in a golden glow.

Still, she still looked pale.

Vulnerable.

"Then take a shower and I'll fix us something to eat. I want to get an early start at the cabin."

She shivered, then grabbed her robe, tugged it on, and slid from bed. "I'll go with you. If Thad's body is on that land, I need to know."

Maddox gave a clipped nod, then strode from the room, ignoring the pull of attraction he felt for her.

He had a job to do and he damned well better get to it.

His brothers would be coming to Pistol Whip any day now to see their dying father, and he wanted this case tied up first. It would take all his energy to deal with them.

ROSE STEPPED BENEATH the warm spray of water, hoping the shower could wash away the last disturbing memory of that nightmare. But the tune from that music box continued to haunt her.

Maybe she'd seen a box like it in her antiques business. When she'd first decided to set up the store, she'd traveled across Wyoming, even visited a few other states, in search of unique items to add to her inventory.

Furniture brought in the bigger bucks, but some rare items with history behind them were valuable.

But it wasn't the money that drew her to the business. It was the history of family and memories associated with the items. Those were the priceless parts she wanted to pass on to her customers. The value of a cigar humidor that had originated with a general in World War II who'd passed it down to his son, who'd then handed it down to his son. A rare coin found in a fire dating back to the 1800s. An antique belt buckle engraved with a family crest. A piece of jewelry that was passed from mother to daughter to grand-daughter. A rocking chair hand-carved by a craftsman for his wife to rock their infant in.

They were treasures in Rose's eyes.

But her father had discouraged her from getting attached to things. They'd moved from place to place every couple of years, never really making a home, never taking any personal items with them. In fact, twice she remembered waking up in the car when they were on their way to a new town, crying for a favorite doll or stuffed animal they'd forgotten and left behind.

They'd never spoken of her grandparents, aunts, uncles or cousins. It was almost as if they'd cut anyone close to them out of their lives.

The same with friends they'd made in each town. And there had been very few of those.

She rinsed the shampoo and conditioner from her hair, climbed from the shower and dried off. Then she quickly dressed in jeans and a button-down shirt. If they were hiking through the woods in search of a grave or Thad's body, she wanted to dress for it.

She braided her hair and tied it at the nape of her neck, and dabbed on a little powder to mask the dark circles beneath her eyes.

The scent of coffee wafted toward her as she ventured downstairs. She found Maddox in her kitchen, scrambling eggs on the stove with a mug of coffee in one hand.

For a moment, her breath caught. The big, tough-looking cowboy seemed at ease in the kitchen, but his jaw was still set in that firm line, and when he looked up at her, a dark wariness had settled in his eyes.

He poured her a cup of coffee and handed it to her, their fingers brushing. A tingle rippled through her at the heat, but he yanked his hand back quickly and scooped the eggs onto a plate.

"We need to talk."

Rose's instincts surged to life, and she sank into the kitchen chair and sipped her coffee. "You found something?"

He shook his head, then joined her at the table, his big hands wrapped around the mug. "That's just it, Rose. I ran a background check on Thad Thoreau and didn't find anything."

She frowned. "Nothing incriminating?"

"I mean *nothing*," he said, emphasizing the last word. "As in the Thad Thoreau you knew doesn't exist."

MADDOX SIPPED HIS COFFEE, giving Rose time to process what he'd said.

"What do you mean, he doesn't exist?" Rose asked.

"Not on paper." Maddox scooped up a bite of eggs and chewed. "He doesn't show up in the DMV or any of the databases I checked."

"Maybe he went by a middle name?"

"I did an extensive search, Rose. I think he used a fake identity so no one could trace him after he left Pistol Whip."

Rose's face blanched. "You mean, once I was dead."

He nodded, his expression grim. "I sent his photo to the lab. Hopefully their facial recognition software will turn up something."

Rose ran her finger along the rim of her cup. "You must think I'm a complete idiot."

Maddox grunted. "No. I think you're a beautiful woman who trusted the wrong man."

Rose's gaze shot to his. *He thought she was beautiful?*

"Look, Rose, the business card Thoreau gave you was bogus. There's no such company. He created an identity with the sole purpose of getting to know you. Then he seduced you into going with him to an isolated place so he could kill you and no one would know. By the time someone in town realized you were missing, he'd be long gone, probably living under another name."

ROSE STARED OUT the window as they drove to Cheyenne, where Maddox dropped off the forensics at the lab.

Nerves gathered in her stomach as they left.

"Thank you for not mentioning my involvement," Rose said wryly.

Maddox darted a furtive look at her. "I want the facts,

the truth," he said matter-of-factly. "Not being able to find Thoreau in the databases raises suspicions about his activity and motives in itself. It also adds credence to your story. No sense bringing in other authorities until we know more."

Rose twined her hands together, grateful that he believed her. But would another law officer accept her story so easily if she had to face charges?

Memories of meeting Thad flashed back. She'd first met him at her store. He'd been friendly and charming, but hadn't stayed in town long. A week later she'd run into him in a restaurant at the hotel where she'd been staying in Cheyenne on a buying trip. It had seemed like serendipity.

He was attentive, flattering, had flirted outrageously with her, and they'd gone to dinner. She'd wound up staying for the weekend and they'd gone sightseeing, had a picnic in the park and attended a concert.

The next few weeks he'd romanced her with phone calls and late-night dinners. That he didn't have family, and she was estranged from her parents, had drawn them together.

But all of it had been a lie.

Maddox turned down the dirt road leading to the cabin, and the memory of Thad closing his hand over hers and telling her he loved her floated back...

Just think, tomorrow you'll be my wife," he murmured as they parked. Rain was threatening, and he rushed around to her side of the car, scooped her into his arms and carried her to the door. They laughed when he nearly slipped on the steps and dropped her.

"I'm going to take a bubble bath," she said after they went inside.

She daydreamed about their wedding as she soaked in the tub.

Then she dried off and tiptoed to the door. She heard Thad's voice and realized he was on the phone...then everything had gone wrong...

How had she missed the signs?

Maddox parked, then retrieved his flashlight from the trunk and pulled on a pair of gloves. Rose followed him, scanning the property in case Thad had survived and was hiding, ready to ambush them.

MADDOX MOTIONED FOR Rose to wait while he searched the house one more time. He'd hoped that he'd missed something the night before, but the place was just as they'd left it, and he still couldn't find any evidence that Thoreau had been shot.

Not even blood or a hair fiber.

The cleanup reeked of a professional job just as he'd originally thought.

When he returned to the porch, Rose was waiting, her expression tormented. "Did you find anything?"

"No, nothing. I'll check the property and woods now."

"I'll go with you," Rose said.

Maddox narrowed his eyes. "You don't have to do that, Rose."

"Two pairs of eyes have to be better than one." She descended the steps, tugging her jacket around her. "Where should we look first?"

"Let's walk around the outside of the house in case there's a crawl space he could have taken refuge in."

Rose took the flashlight he offered, and he strode to the right of the house while she went left.

He passed the side windows, then noticed a storm cellar hidden by overgrown bushes. Suspicion kicking in, he raked weeds aside. The lock was old and rusted and didn't appear to have been opened recently, but he retrieved bolt cutters from his trunk and snapped it.

Dust and cobwebs assaulted him as he pried up the lid and shone the light inside. A rancid odor hit him, swirling upward, and he had to turn his head and take a deep breath to stifle a reaction.

He clenched the flashlight, then removed his gun from his holster and held it at the ready as he slowly inched down the steps. He coughed as dust floated upward, and the wood step creaked, a rung snapping with his weight. He aimed the light around the interior of the shelter, noting a wall of shelves filled with canned goods that had probably been there for years.

On the ground, bags of what looked like flour and sugar had been ripped open and dug through by animals.

But the skeleton in the corner stopped him cold. Decay had eroded the body, the eye sockets bulging, the bones a dull gray.

Dammit, he'd thought he might find Thoreau, but this body had been here for a long time.

Who the hell was it?

Chapter Seven

Rose surveyed the outside of the cabin, searching for a crawl space or any other place a body could be left, but found nothing. Wind stirred the dust around her, sending twigs flying across the dry land. In spite of the chill in the air, nerves made perspiration dampen her clothes as she walked back to the underground storm cellar.

Maddox emerged, wiping dirt from his face, his eyes stormy.

"You found Thad?"

"No," he said. "But there's a skeleton down there in that pit."

Rose's breath caught. "What? Who is it?"

His massive shoulders lifted into a shrug. "I don't know. It's been down there for a while." He lifted his cowboy hat and wiped his face with the back of his hand. "I'll have to call the sheriff in Cheyenne and report this."

Rose's lungs strained for air. If he called in other law enforcement, he'd have to explain about Thad.

"I want to search the property first," Maddox said. "Then we'll know what we're dealing with."

Rose's mind raced. He thought there might be more than one skeleton on the property.

And who did the remains in the storm cellar belong to? Had Thad known the remains were there?

The fact that he'd brought her here to kill her might mean that he'd murdered before...

Maddox gestured toward the woods leading to the creek, and she followed him through the brush. "Should we split up?"

Maddox shook his head. "No, stay with me."

Rose didn't like the hard look in his eyes. Did he want her with him because he was afraid Thad or the other man might be here hiding out, ready to pounce on them? Or because he didn't trust her?

FINDING THAT SKELETON didn't sit well with Maddox. Dammit, if Thoreau had succeeded in killing Rose, he could have left her body in that cellar to rot just like the other man, and no one would have ever known.

He'd have to call in a forensic specialist to identify the skeleton and determine cause of death. Knowing that might lead him to his killer.

The even bigger question—was his death connected to Rose?

He surveyed the ground studying the weeds, dry grass, scrub brush and bushes, searching for any sign that the land had been recently disturbed.

An animal skittered across the woods, and Rose startled.

His senses alert, he scanned the area.

"It was a prairie dog," he said as he spotted the animal running through the weeds.

He spent the next half hour scrutinizing the land, inch by inch, pausing to examine loose clumps of dirt and patches of weeds that might indicate footprints or foul play. He found the remains of an animal's carcass that had been mauled and ravaged, but no human remains.

The wind picked up, clouding the air with dust, and he stumbled over a tree stump and some branches a few feet from the creek. A group of stones were piled in one spot, drawing his gaze to them.

Rose hovered behind him. "What is it?"

He yanked away the smaller stones, then the larger one. "I don't know, we'll see." Using a stick, he dug away the dirt, his skin crawling, when a few inches in, the stick hit bone.

Using his hands he brushed away more dirt, dread settling in the pit of his stomach. The skeleton of a person's hand was poking through the dirt.

"OH, MY GOD," Rose said in a choked whisper. "There's someone buried here."

"It looks that way."

Rose's stomach lurched. "Do you think it's Thad?"

Maddox shook his head. "No, it's just bones."

Rose's insides quivered as she studied the stones that Maddox had moved aside to unearth the remains "If the same person killed both of these people, why bury one and not the other?"

"Good question." Maddox brushed his hands together to shake off the dirt. "They could have been put here at different times."

The wind picked up, swirling leaves and loose twigs around her feet as she looked around them. What was this place, some kind of makeshift graveyard for a killer's victims?

You could have been among them.

The thought nauseated her.

"Under the circumstances, I'd better call the sheriff in Cheyenne. We need a team to search and make sure there aren't more skeletons here."

"You think Thad knew about these?"

"I don't know." Maddox's jaw tightened. "If he did, it

means he's connected to these deaths. Finding out their identities may lead us to more information about him."

And her.

She heard the unspoken words and understood.

"Thad could be a hired killer, Rose. If so, murdering you wasn't personal to Thoreau. The person who hired him had the motive."

She jammed her hands on her hips. "I can't imagine why anyone would want me dead."

Maddox narrowed his eyes. "You can't think of anyone who might want to hurt you?"

Rose shook her head, baffled. "I run an antiques store," she said. "I don't have a lot of money."

"No siblings?"

"No."

"Anyone jealous of your business?"

"It's a small town, Maddox. You know that. Who would be intimidated by my store in Pistol Whip?"

He narrowed his eyes. "What about old boyfriends before Thoreau?"

Rose made a self-deprecating sound. "There weren't any. At least no one serious."

"Did your parents have any enemies?"

Rose sighed. "Not that I know of. They're not exactly rich. And they kept to themselves. No enemies but no real close friends, either."

"No big business ventures or investments?"

"No. They lived paycheck to paycheck."

Maddox removed his phone from the clip on his belt and punched in a number. "This is Sheriff Maddox McCullen from Pistol Whip. I'm on some property in your jurisdiction and found skeletal remains. Send a crime team and ME, ASAP." A pause. "Yes, I'll text you the coordinates."

He ended the call and sent the text, and Rose walked

down to the creek and stared into the muddy water as she waited for the crime team.

Anxiety filled her though. Telling her story again would be difficult. But she had to know the truth about Thad and the skeletons they'd found.

After all, she could have been one of them.

MADDOX GRIMACED. FINDING REMAINS on the land where Rose's fiancé/attacker had planned to leave her body couldn't be coincidental.

But how were they related? She didn't seem to know they were here, claimed to have no enemies and appeared to have no idea why Thoreau planned to kill her.

He started toward her, but twigs snapped to the right, and he jerked his head sideways. A shadow flickered in the corner of his eye, and he noted movement. An animal or…Thoreau?

Gripping his weapon, he studied the area and saw more movement. Bushes parted. Bugs swarmed, and a vulture circled above, its talons bared as it swooped toward the ground.

Another body? Maybe Thoreau?

He inched toward the sound, eyes peeled for trouble. A rancid stench hit him, and he covered his mouth to keep from gagging. He yanked his handkerchief from his pocket, covered his mouth and breathed out. Then he forged on, shoving weeds and bramble aside as he plowed through the wooded area.

The smell grew more acrid as he neared the spot where the vulture circled. The trees were so thick it looked dark so he shined his light through the weeds, searching for Thoreau in the scrub brush.

His foot hit something and he stumbled, then looked

down, half expecting to see another grave. A dead coyote lay at his feet, his insides mangled and spilling out.

Twigs cracked, the wind whistled shrilly off the mountains and the swish of brush parting echoed behind him. His fingers tightened around his gun, and he started to jerk around, but before he could, something hard slammed into the back of his skull.

A sharp pain wracked him and the world tilted, then spun. He fought the dizziness, tried to grab hold of a tree limb to keep upright, but another blow landed and his knees buckled.

He collapsed into the dirt, struggling to remain conscious. He had to protect Rose, warn her...

But the darkness swallowed him.

ROSE HEARD A NOISE, the sound of something thrashing behind her.

She'd left Maddox standing by the grave, but she couldn't see him now. Suddenly nervous, she turned and scanned the area. He was probably continuing his search.

Just the thought of the remains he'd discovered made her shudder with fear and revulsion. Another noise jerked her attention to the left, and she saw a deer running through the woods.

A deep sigh of relief escaped her, and she told herself she was being paranoid. Still, she couldn't see Maddox, so she walked toward the grave, calling Maddox's name again.

Leaves rustled, and she stumbled over a tree stump as she hurried her pace. She had to find Maddox. He wouldn't leave her out here alone.

But the air behind her suddenly changed, and she felt someone behind her. Praying it was Maddox, she started to whirl around, but a hard whack on her head sent her to the ground. She caught herself with her hands, her knees slamming into a rock, the world turning to gray as two hands grabbed her and a fist slammed against the side of her head.

She tried to scream, but the sound died as she fell face-first into the dirt.

She struggled to keep from passing out, but she was too weak and disoriented to move. Her attacker grabbed her under the arms, and dragged her through the bramble. Weeds and dry grass clawed at her body, rocks gouging her, a trickle of blood seeping down her forehead.

She tried to fight, but she couldn't make her limbs work, and she couldn't see anything but the distant fog of trees passing and the wings of a vulture swooping down as if it was diving for her.

They crossed the driveway, the gravel and rocks beating at her as he continued to drag her, then a creaking sound echoed above the howl of the wind. He released her for just a second, and she struggled to roll to her knees so she could get up, but he kicked her in the back, sending pain rocketing through her lower extremities.

While she was still trying to recover from the blow, he shoved her forward.

Dear God. The creaking sound had been the door to the storm cellar opening. She let out a scream, but he shoved her through the opening and tossed her down into the darkness.

She screamed again and tasted dirt as she fell on her hands and knees, then collapsed, her face hitting the ground. Terror streaked through her as she looked up and saw the skeleton in the corner.

Whoever had attacked her was going to leave her here to die in the dark, to rot like the dead man they'd just found.

A second later, a faint light spilled through the opening above. Then she screamed again, as Maddox's body fell into the hole and landed with a loud crunch beside her.

DAMN ROSE FOR escaping the first time. She seemed to have a knack for that. She'd fought off Thoreau and then gone to the local sheriff.

The bitch had to die.

She had lived too long already.

With every day that passed, he feared her memory would return. That she'd recall where she'd first seen him.

Then she would destroy his family.

But he wouldn't let that happen.

Rose should have died twenty years ago. She'd been a problem ever since. But now that he'd found her, he would extinguish the problem for good.

And his secrets would go with her to the grave.

Chapter Eight

Panic seized Rose. Blood matted the hair on the back of Maddox's head. And he was so still…

The scent of decay and dank earth overwhelmed her, and she swallowed back nausea at the sight of the empty eye sockets of the skeleton. It seemed to be staring at her, accusing, as if she was somehow responsible for letting him rot away down here alone.

Had he been dead when he'd been thrown down here? Or had he been alive? He could have starved to death, grown dehydrated, tried to claw his way out until finally he realized no one was coming to save him.

She dragged in a shaky breath, her resolve kicking in. She wouldn't just lie here and die.

She had to find a way to get her and Maddox out of this hole.

She listened for sounds that her attacker was still up there, but she didn't hear anything for a second. Wiping dirt from her face, she pushed herself to a sitting position, steadied her breathing, and crawled over to Maddox. He was laying facedown, one arm flung above his head, the other by his side.

Her heart pounding, she pulled up the back of his shirt to make sure he hadn't been shot. His back felt cool to her touch, alarming her, and his breathing was shallow.

"Maddox, please talk to me," she whispered. "I need you to be okay."

But he remained still, his body limp.

She ran her fingers along the wound on his head, gauging its length and depth. About three inches long, maybe a quarter-inch deep. He could use stitches, but it wasn't deep enough to be life-threatening.

She ripped off the bottom of her T-shirt, tore a section from it and folded it to press over his wound to stem the blood flow. Then she tied the strip around his head, making sure to pad the injury and tighten it enough to hold the makeshift blood stopper in place. He moaned and stirred slightly, and she brushed his cheek with her fingers. "We're going to get out of here," Rose said in a hoarse voice. "I promise, Maddox. I'll find a way."

She gently shook him, hoping to rouse him. "Maddox, can you hear me?"

A low grunt and he moved one finger, but lapsed back into unconsciousness. Frustrated, she felt his jacket, searching for his phone, but she didn't find it.

Panic set in. She'd left her phone in the car.

A surge of anger swamped Rose, and she stood on wobbly legs and ran her hands along the wall to the rickety stairs that led upward. She grabbed the rungs, splinters jabbing into her palms from the rotting wood as she pulled herself up onto the first one.

Slowly she climbed to the next one, blowing out dust that rained down through the crack above. Her foot slid and she almost fell to the bottom, but she managed to dig her hands in and hang on.

Another rung cracked, the wood giving way, but she latched onto the one above it and dragged herself to the next one. Two more, and her head hit the wood board covering the opening. She held on with one hand and pushed at the door, but it was firmly in place.

She shoved and pushed again, using all her force, but it wouldn't budge. Then she heard a noise above her, and felt the door bow slightly.

Horror filled her as she realized the man who'd shoved her down here had just moved something big and heavy on top of the door to prevent their escape.

MADDOX GROANED AT the throbbing pain in his head. A hammer was pounding at his temple.

He tried to open his eyelids, but they felt weighted and so did his arms and legs. He heaved for a breath and inhaled dirt, coughing as dust clogged his throat. Where the hell was he?

He blinked to clear his vision, but it was too damn dark to see. The creak of wood splintering erupted, then a woman's shriek punctuated the air. He slowly pushed up enough to turn his head in the direction of the sound and a sliver of light peeked through just enough for him to see.

Rose.

Reality crashed back as his memory returned. He'd found the remains of two people on the property, but someone had assaulted him from behind. "Rose?"

She pushed up from the ground and crawled toward him. "Maddox, you're all right?"

He felt like hell, but he murmured that he was. "What happened?"

"Someone attacked me. He threw me down in this cellar, and then he dumped you here, too."

The cellar? The skeleton...

Dammit. He lifted a hand and felt the back of his head. A rag was tied around his head. His fingers touched something sticky. *Blood.*

Rose stroked his hair from his forehead. "You're hurt, Maddox. I tried to stop the bleeding."

"Don't worry about me, Rose. I've had worse." He struggled to sit up. Rose grabbed his arm to help him, but his head spun, and he was so dizzy he had to lower his head in his hands for a few minutes until the feeling subsided.

Rose trembled beside him, and he forced his eyes open. "Are you okay?"

"Yes," Rose whispered. "Just a little bruised."

"Did you see who attacked you?"

"No, he came up behind me," she said in a strained voice. "I was standing by the creek, and I heard a noise and I turned to find you, but I couldn't see you. Then I started to look for you, but…he came up behind me and hit me."

Maddox hated the fear in her voice, but she had reason to be afraid.

"Did you see him?" Rose asked.

"No. He attacked me from behind, too." He blinked her back into focus, his eyes finally adjusting to the darkness.

Her breath rattled in the tension-filled air. "I climbed the stairs, but I couldn't push open the door. I think he put something heavy on it to make sure we couldn't get out."

Maddox heaved a frustrated breath, then reached for her hand and pulled her close to him. "We will get out of here, I promise."

He raked his other hand across the ground. "My gun… do you see it?"

Rose crawled around to look for it, feeling the ground and then searching near the steps. "No. It's not here."

"Dammit, the bastard probably took it. How about my phone?"

"I already checked. Either he took it or you lost it up there. And mine is in the car."

Anger fueled Maddox's adrenaline. "I called the Cheyenne sheriff before I was hit, Rose. He should be here soon."

"But what if he doesn't find us?" Rose said in a panicked whisper.

Maddox squeezed her hand. "Listen to me. He knows I'm here because I told him I'd wait on him. He'll see my car, and he's bringing a team with him to search the premises as well as remove the skeletons. He'll find us."

ROSE FORCED HERSELF not to look at the bones in the corner. Maddox's arms around her felt comforting, his calm voice soothing her fears. All they had to do was wait. Help was on its way.

Except as the minutes passed, she felt as if she couldn't breathe. The dirt walls were closing in around her, the air was stale, hot, and reeked of a putrid odor. Death and decay.

"I've been thinking about that girl on the milk carton," Maddox said. "And the reason Thoreau thought you were her."

"It makes no sense," Rose whispered.

Maddox exhaled. "Rose, is it possible you were adopted?"

Something tickled Rose's leg. A spider. She hated spiders.

Frantic, she shook her foot, brushing it off with her hand. "No. I mean, I don't think so."

Maddox rubbed a finger along her arm to calm her. "What's your earliest memory of your family?"

Rose closed her eyes, struggling to recall. "Christmas," Rose said. "I remember decorating the tree with candy canes and watching my mom and dad string lights on our porch."

"How old were you?"

"Four? Five?" Rose rubbed her forehead. "What are you getting at?"

Maddox ran a finger over the scar at her temple. "You touch that scar all the time. How did you get it?"

"I don't remember," she said. "My parents said we were in an accident, a car crash when I was little."

Maddox seemed quiet for a moment. "You don't recall it?"

"No. I had a concussion."

Maddox cleared his throat. "You mentioned that you and your parents moved around a lot?"

"We did," Rose said. "My father kept changing jobs."

"Did you ever take on a new name?"

Rose shook her head, but the hair on the back of her neck prickled. "No. Why would you ask that?"

Maddox shrugged. "Just thinking about that milk carton photo and trying to figure out why Thoreau thought it was you."

Rose's stomach tightened. "You think I was adopted, that something happened to my birth parents?"

"It might explain things."

"But the Worthingtons have pictures of me as a baby. Pictures of when I took my first step, ate my first solid foods."

Maddox murmured a low sound. "Could you have had a sister that you don't know about? Maybe a twin?"

Rose worried her bottom lip with her teeth. "I don't know. Maybe." Questions pummeled her. "But if I did, why wouldn't my folks have told me about her? And why would someone want to kill me or that girl?"

"I don't know, Rose. I could speculate, but I'd rather get more information first. Maybe Thoreau mistook you for another girl. If we find out who the girl on the milk carton was and why she was missing, it might lead us to the truth."

"I guess I need to have a conversation with my parents."

Rose twisted her hands together. But voices sounded above, and Maddox jumped up and staggered toward the steps.

He banged on the ceiling door. "We're down here!"

Rose followed his lead and began to shout so the team

above could hear them. But Maddox's questions about her family taunted her.

Surely her parents would have told her if she was adopted or had a sister.

Wouldn't they?

MADDOX POUNDED ON the board above them. "Down here!'

Dust fluttered through the cracks of the board as he beat on it, then a voice called out. "Hang on, we'll get you out."

Movement sounded above, and he coaxed Rose aside while the team pried the door open.

Seconds later, the board was lifted and blessed sunshine seeped inside. He took Rose's hand. "Go on, Rose, you first."

Rose allowed him to help her up the ladder, and he followed, drinking in fresh air as they climbed from the cellar.

"Sheriff Jarvis," the big guy said as he tipped his Stetson. He gestured toward a young woman wearing dark glasses with her hair pulled back in a tight bun. "This is the medical examiner and state forensic specialist, Dr. Lail." A younger man in a deputy's uniform appeared, his thin face set in a scowl. A group of crime scene investigators piled out of a van. "And this is my deputy, Warner Rogers." He gestured toward Maddox's head. "Either of you need a medic?"

"No, I'm fine," Maddox said, then gently touched Rose's arm. "Rose?"

She shook her head. "No, I'm okay."

But she wasn't okay and they both knew it. She was terrified and they still had no answers.

Sheriff Jarvis crossed his arms. "Mind telling me how you came across these remains?"

Maddox sighed and explained about Thoreau.

"I was looking for him when we checked this cellar and I found the first skeleton."

The sheriff motioned to his deputy. "Start searching the area. Let's make certain there aren't any other skeletons out here."

Chapter Nine

Rose remained by the creek while Maddox, the sheriff and the crime scene workers began to process the area. They combed the property and woods, and searched in a four-mile radius up and down the creek bank.

Thankfully they found no other remains. Dr. Lail emerged from the pit, and yanked off her latex gloves.

"What can you tell us from your preliminary exam?" Maddox asked.

Dr. Lail adjusted her glasses. "The skeleton in the storm cellar belongs to a male, Caucasian. At one time, he sustained a bad break to his femur and has pins in his leg. I'll let you know more after I examine the bones more closely."

Maddox turned to one of the CSIs. "Did you find any forensics? A bullet casing?"

"Found a bullet casing indicating he might have been shot, some hair fibers, and a loose button," the female CSI said. "We'll keep you posted once we process them."

Dr. Lail went to look at the remains they'd uncovered in the ground. Rose followed, her stomach turning.

"This body belongs to a female," Dr. Lail says. "I say she's been dead about the same amount of time as the man in that cellar."

"Why bury one and leave the other body trapped down there?" Maddox asked.

Dr. Lail shrugged. "Who knows? Maybe the killer planned to bury both of them and ran out of time."

Maddox contemplated different scenarios. "Or the man showed up when the killer was burying the woman, so he shot him and threw him in the hole while he finished burying her."

"How long will it take to examine the bones?" Jarvis asked.

Dr. Lail tugged the sheet up over the body and gestured for the CSI team to load it in the van. "I'll get on it right away."

"Thanks," Maddox interjected when Sheriff Jarvis started to speak. "It's possible these deaths are connected to the person who tried to kill Ms. Worthington."

"Then it goes to the top of my list," Dr. Lail said.

Maddox thanked her, and Rose watched as the team closed the back of the van and drove away.

Sheriff Jarvis gave her a curious look but directed his comment to Maddox. "Fill out a report on what transpired here and send it to me."

"I'll write it up," Maddox said. "But for now, let's keep the investigation quiet. It might work to our advantage to let the perpetrator think he got away with killing me and Rose."

NIGHT WAS FALLING as Rose climbed into Maddox's car and they left the gruesome scene. Maddox had explained Rose's situation, but Sheriff Jarvis insisted on hearing her version of the story.

Telling it again drove home the fear that had swept over her at Thad's betrayal.

She wasn't sure if Sheriff Jarvis believed her, but having Maddox on her side helped. Besides, Jarvis couldn't arrest her for murder when they had no evidence that Thad was dead.

"I think we need to talk to your parents," Maddox said.

Rose's heart stuttered. The last time they'd spoken had been nearly a year ago.

For years, they'd smothered her, not allowed her to have friends over to visit, had discouraged her from participating in school events and athletics. Once, she'd excelled on the track team, even catching the attention of the local press, but they'd forbidden her from attending the championship meet and denied the reporter the story.

And now she was going to confront them about the possibility that she was adopted. She could just imagine their reaction.

"You want to call them?" Maddox asked.

Rose contemplated their reunion. In light of the fact that she could have died, she should appreciate her family. But nerves gripped her stomach.

Still, if they knew anything about the picture or the reason Thad thought she was that missing little girl, she had to talk to them.

"I can't. I don't have their current number."

"What do you mean?"

"They only used prepaid cell phones."

"You never thought that was odd?"

Rose shrugged. "I just assumed it was their way of limiting the minutes to save money."

"Where do they live?" Maddox asked once she'd disconnected the call.

"Cheyenne."

"Then we'll drive over."

MADDOX PHONED HOME while Rose washed up at the barbecue restaurant. Mama Mary answered on the second ring. "How's Dad?"

Mama Mary sighed into the phone. "He's resting now,

but he's had a rough day. He asked if you'd talked to your brothers."

Maddox gritted his teeth. "I called Brett and Ray and explained about Dad's condition. Hopefully they'll be home in a few days."

Although he wasn't counting on it. Brett was hooked on fame and had too many women in his bed to want to leave them. And Ray...Ray had always been obstinate, angry, resentful.

Maddox had never understood it.

"Tell Dad I'm working an investigation, but I'll be home when I can."

"I will, Maddox," Mama Mary said, her voice worried. "I just hope your brothers come home before it's too late."

Maddox's chest clenched as she hung up. But his phone buzzed, and he checked the caller ID screen. The lab.

He punched Connect. "Sheriff McCullen."

"Maddox, it's Devon. I ran that blood you brought in. Type AB negative. The partial print was inconclusive—I'm afraid I didn't find a match, although if you bring me one for comparison, I might be able to do better."

Frustration knotted the muscles in his neck. "Thanks, Devon. Isn't AB negative a rare blood type?"

"Yes, one out of one hundred people have it."

"Devon, can you search for donors or recipients of that blood type the last few months?" It was a long shot, but something might pop.

"Sure. It'll take time, though."

"Also, check military and criminal records. The name Thoreau didn't show up in the databases I checked but he was probably using an assumed name. If he was trained as a sniper, or committed murder before, we might get lucky and find his real ID using that blood type."

ROSE FIDGETED. Had her parents constantly changed phones to keep someone from finding them?

"Tell me more about the Worthingtons," Maddox said as they drove.

"They're homebodies. Although we moved around, once we got to a new place, they settled in. They didn't entertain, we didn't go out and they never got involved in social activities with neighbors or my school. In fact, when I won an award for track and a reporter wanted to interview me, they insisted I quit the team and forbade me from joining any other clubs."

Maddox gave her an odd look, his brows raised. "How about other family? Grandparents? Aunts and uncles or cousins?"

"They said my grandparents were dead. And they never mentioned any other family."

"You said you moved around a lot?"

Rose fidgeted. "Yes. I hated it. Just when I'd start making friends, we'd pick up and go, usually with no warning."

Maddox scrubbed a hand through his hair. "Did they ever seem nervous when you were in public? Maybe paranoid, as if they thought they were being followed?"

The air around Rose seemed to fill with tension. "What? Why would you ask that?"

"Did they?"

Rose inhaled sharply. "Maybe a few times. My dad used to check the rearview mirror a lot. And come to think of it, when we went to a restaurant, he always went to the back and sat facing the door so he could see if anyone came in."

"Hmm."

"What are you thinking?"

"I'm just wondering if they might have been in WITSEC?"

Rose's pulse stuttered. "Witness protection?"

"Yes. It would explain why they moved a lot. They

could have witnessed a crime and gone into hiding to keep you safe."

Rose lapsed into a thoughtful silence. "I guess that would explain why they discouraged me from making friends and being interviewed for the paper."

He nodded. "Although usually people in WITSEC change identities with each move."

Rose's fingers lifted to the scar at her temple, a faint memory tickling her mind. *Someone calling her Amber... no, Annabelle? No, Helen or...*

The name was on the tip of her tongue, but it eluded her.

"Did any strange men or women come around, maybe someone who looked official, like a cop or marshal?"

She looked out the window at the land passing, the headlights bouncing off the ruts in the road. "Not that I remember. In fact..." Another memory plucked at her.

"What?"

"Both my parents hated the police," Rose admitted. "Dad said they used their power to get what they wanted. In fact, once an officer visited to talk about safety and fingerprint the kids in our class, but my parents kept me home that day."

Was Maddox right? Could her parents have been afraid for their lives and been on the run?

Rose perked up at the sight of the familiar market on the corner of the neighborhood where her parents lived. It was an older development with ranch houses catering to the middle class. Nondescript. Nothing too shabby, but nothing showy, either.

That had always been their motto.

Don't draw attention to yourself. Be a quiet little worker bee and never make noise.

At the time, she'd interpreted it to mean that they were embarrassed by her.

"Turn at the corner," Rose said, anxious at the thought

of seeing them again. How would they react to her surprise visit? Would they welcome her with loving arms? Or be furious at her questions?

"Which house belongs to your folks?" Maddox asked.

"The split-level at the end on the left."

Night shadows plagued the streets and yards, and a streetlight had burned out, leaving the last three houses in darkness. She leaned forward, her pulse quickening at the sight of the black sedan in the drive. Her father had always driven a black sedan, never anything else. At one point, she'd actually overheard her parents arguing about that—her mother wanted a shiny new red SUV, but her father had balked, saying that red cars attracted attention they didn't need.

At the time she hadn't thought much of it, only that her father was so conservative, he should have been born in a different era. Now...she wondered if there was another reason he hadn't wanted anyone to notice them.

Maddox steered the car into the drive, a frown pulling at his face. "The lights are off in the front of the house. It doesn't look like they're home."

Rose checked her watch. "It's only nine. They usually go to bed at ten."

"Maybe they're out?"

"I told you, my parents never go out." Rose reached for the door handle. "We've come this far. We might as well see if they're inside." Although as they approached the house, a sense of doom overwhelmed Rose.

Maddox kept glancing around the perimeter, his movements cautious, as if he sensed trouble.

This was her parents' home, she reminded herself. *For God's sake.* Her boring, sensible, sometimes difficult, smothering parents who had practically locked her away from friends and other kids because they were loners... no, once her mother *had* said it was to keep her safe.

She'd thought her mother was just being overprotective.

But…what if they had been in trouble?

She knocked gently on the front door, but the house seemed quiet. No one was moving inside. No lights flicking on. Only a low light burned faintly through the sheers from the bedroom to the right.

Her parents' room.

She reached for the front door to open it, but Maddox threw up a warning hand and gestured for her to step behind him.

"Shh," Maddox said. He pushed the door open, his boots squeaking on the parquet floor as he entered.

"They always lock the door," Rose whispered.

Maddox nodded, then pulled his gun at the ready. She gaped at him, but bit her tongue. How could she argue with him for being careful after what they'd been through?

The foyer was dark, the sound of the clock ticking in the hallway reverberating in the silence.

"Mom? Dad?" Rose called.

No answer.

Maddox inched farther inside, and they glanced in the den. Nothing. The *drip, drip, drip* of a faucet echoed from the bathroom, and he gestured that he was going to check the bedroom.

Rose held her breath as they crept down the hall.

The moment they reached the doorway, a throbbing took root in Rose's chest.

Her parents were sprawled on the floor, facedown, blood pooled around them.

Chapter Ten

Rose gasped. This couldn't be happening. Her parents couldn't be…dead.

"Don't touch anything," Maddox murmured.

Rose pressed her sweaty palms to her mouth and stared at her mother and father in shock.

Maddox shot her a sympathetic look, then coaxed her back toward the door. "Wait out here, Rose. Don't touch anything."

She bent over at the waist, drawing in a breath, and he rubbed her back until she calmed. "Go to the kitchen. Let me handle this."

She shook her head, but then gripped the wall. "I can't believe this. Why…?"

He let the question stand. He didn't have the answers now, but he would find them.

Maddox inched closer to the bodies, careful not to touch anything as he snapped pictures with his cell phone. "It appears they both died from a gunshot wound to the back of the head. It looks professional, Rose."

Shock rolled through Rose. Her last conversation with her mother replayed in her head. Her father had been livid that she'd posted her picture on a social media site. She'd tried to explain that she'd only done so to make business contacts for Vintage Treasures, but he'd ordered her to take it down. Her mother had jumped in to agree…

"I'm an adult now," Rose said. *"I'm tired of hiding out from the world. I can't be a hermit like you."*

Then her mother probed her about her friends and lovers. Rose drew the line and told them to let her lead her own life.

"It's not safe out there," her father said.

Rose was sick of his overprotectiveness. "If it were up to you, I'd live in a bubble. But it's not up to you anymore..."

Not safe? Had he known she was in danger? That someone would look for her and try to hurt her?

"I need to call the local police and get a crime team," Maddox said. "I doubt the killer left any forensics, but I have to go by the book."

Rose nodded, a numbness spreading over as grief engulfed her. She would never get to talk to her parents again, never spend another holiday with them, never...get to tell them she was sorry for the way they'd argued.

For not calling to check on them in the last year.

Maddox punched in a number, and she heard him explaining about finding her parents.

As he hung up, he crossed to her and rubbed her arms with his hands. "Rose, are you okay?"

She shook her head, emotions choking her. "How can I be okay? Someone killed my family, and...it's probably the same person who tried to kill me." She looked into his eyes, searching for answers even though she knew he had none yet.

"Trust me, Rose. We will find out who did this," Maddox said, his voice filled with conviction.

She gripped his hands to steady herself and nodded. She believed him. But finding the killer wouldn't bring back her parents.

Even if they had the answers she needed, it was too late now.

MADDOX SILENTLY CURSED at this turn of events. He'd hoped to hell Rose's parents would be able to fill in the holes regarding Thoreau and the picture on the milk carton.

But someone had gotten to them first.

He inched closer to the couple and stooped down to study the bodies. A single gunshot wound to the back of the temple. Execution style.

Exactly as a professional hit man would do.

The stench of death permeated the room, indicating the couple had been dead for hours.

Had the killer murdered the Worthingtons, then driven to the cabin to sabotage him and Rose?

Or were they dealing with two different perpetrators?

Rose sank onto the edge of the bed, her complexion ashen. Maddox glanced around the room to see if anything had been disturbed, but nothing was visible. The killer hadn't bothered to make this look like a robbery gone bad.

Still, he was surprised there hadn't been a struggle.

"I'm going to look around before the crime team gets here." Maddox kneeled in front of Rose. "Rose?"

Her eyes looked tormented as she looked up at him. "Why would he kill them? They were just an ordinary couple—just like I'm ordinary."

Maddox gritted his teeth. He had a sinking feeling that statement was far from the truth. "If they were in WITSEC like we discussed before, maybe they could identify him."

"But if we were in WITSEC, why would my face be on a milk carton as if I was missing?"

"Good question." Maddox didn't like the immediate answer that came to mind. That the Worthingtons had been criminals themselves, not just innocent victims or witnesses. That they'd kidnapped Rose.

If so, who were her birth parents? Were they looking for her? And if Thoreau had been hired to find her on behalf of her birth family, why try to kill Rose?

Unless the Worthingtons had kidnapped Rose to protect her from her real family? Perhaps her birth parents were afraid Rose would remember something incriminating about them…

The questions needled him as he searched the dresser. Basic underwear, pajamas and T-shirts filled the drawers. The nightstands held very little—a pack of breath mints, a pencil and a crossword puzzle book that had several puzzles filled out.

Maddox checked the bedroom closet. Slacks and men's shirts lined one side while women's blouses, pants and shoes occupied the opposite. Dark drab colors, plain nondescript shoes, a conservative outdated suit, nothing dressy or showy.

Rose claimed that her parents didn't like to call attention to themselves. He'd bet his best horse that was for a reason.

He searched the top shelf for anything that could shed light on the couple but found nothing but a baseball cap and a rain jacket. He ran his hand along the wall for a safe, but came up empty.

As he emerged from the closet, Rose was sitting so still and looked so damn pale it made his chest clench. "Nothing in there." He paused in front of her and stooped down to her again. "Come on, Rose, why don't you look around the kitchen or the living room while I search the other rooms."

Her breath rushed out as she stood, and she let him lead her to the living room, where she sank onto the couch. "I should have talked to them more," Rose whispered. "Told them I was sorry we didn't get along."

Maddox squeezed her hands. They were icy cold, her body trembling. "Everyone argues with their parents, Rose. I'm sure they knew you loved them."

He quickly searched the living room, the coffee table, the drawers in the end table and the coat closet, but nothing seemed amiss. He visually scanned the bookshelves, noting a collection of various paperbacks, but no family photos. Not even a picture of Rose.

Odd. Most parents chronicled their children's lives as they grew up with photographs. It was almost as if there was nothing personal here at all.

He noted the same thing in the kitchen. No pictures on the fridge. The refrigerator held milk, eggs, condiments, sandwich meat but little else. The freezer was stocked with frozen dinners stacked neatly and alphabetized.

He rummaged through the kitchen drawers looking for business cards, a phone book, notes or bills, and found the electricity and water bill addressed to the couple. Nothing else.

There was no computer or phone, landline or cell. He went back to Rose, worried about her.

The Worthingtons were definitely hiding out.

He bit back the words on the tip of his tongue. They might have died trying to protect Rose.

But…if they had taken Rose as a child, they might have been running to protect themselves from being exposed as kidnappers.

THE NUMBNESS THAT had drained Rose of energy seemed to grow as the crime team and medical examiner arrived. She felt as if she was watching a horror show, except this was no show or movie.

This was her real life.

She watched them dust the house for fingerprints and rifle through her parents' desks, closets and drawers. She wasn't sure what they were looking for, but Maddox oversaw the search, his expression bleak.

He followed the ME to the bedroom and stayed during the exam, then returned to stand by Rose while they moved her parents' bodies to transport them to the morgue.

She wanted to go to her mother and kiss her, tell her how sorry she was that they hadn't been closer, but she couldn't force her legs to work.

Maddox lowered his bulk onto the sofa, spread his legs and braced his arms on his knees. "Rose, is there someone I can call for you? Another family member?"

Rose blinked back tears. "I told you, no other family."

"How about a friend?"

Rose had grown so accustomed to holding herself back emotionally because of her parents that she hadn't developed many friends. She liked Trina, her assistant at Vintage Treasures, but they didn't hang out socially.

"Not really. My coworker is watching the shop for a few more days."

"Did you explain what was going on?"

"No. We…aren't that close." A self-deprecating laugh escaped her. "I guess my parents rubbed off on me."

"You let Thoreau into your life," Maddox said softly.

"And look what a mistake that turned out to be." She searched his face to see if he was judging her, but compassion flickered in his deep brown eyes. She wanted to believe that he didn't see her as a fool, or a freak who couldn't make friends, but self-doubt suffused her.

"Your parents didn't have a computer?" Maddox asked.

"Not that I know of."

"Not even for your father's work?"

Rose frowned. "He might have had one at the office, but he didn't bring it home."

"What was the name of the company where he worked?"

"Jensen's Freight and Trucking," Rose said.

"Did you meet his coworkers or boss? Did your family ever socialize with them?"

"No. Dad never even talked about work." *Of course she hadn't thought much about that, either—until now.* "My parents always kept suitcases packed in the closet, so they could leave quickly. Did you find them?"

Maddox stood. "No, I didn't see them. But I'd like to examine their car."

Rose pushed to her feet, a surge of anger sparking her adrenaline. "I'll get the keys." She walked to the bench by the door where her mother always left her handbag.

She dug out the keys and handed them to him, then noticed her mother's wallet. Her fingers shook as she flipped it open and studied her mother's drivers' license. Like most people's, it was a terrible picture. Her mother's muddy brown hair had been pulled back at the nape of her neck, her complexion pale with no makeup, her reading glasses perched on the tip of her nose.

Another trivial thing they'd argued about. Rose had suggested her mother have a makeover, but Ramona had refused, saying she didn't want strange men looking at her, that she was happy with herself.

"How old were your parents?" Maddox asked.

"In their fifties," Rose said. "Too young to die."

Maddox's gaze met hers, the sympathy in his eyes moving her near tears.

The keys jangled in his hand. "Did your parents only have one car?"

"Yes," Rose said. "My mother drove Dad to work when he was taking a long haul in the truck, so she wouldn't be without a car. He worried about us needing it in case of an emergency."

"Come on, Rose. Let's get some air and examine your parents' car."

She nodded, desperate to escape the grisly scene in her house.

She might have had her differences with her parents, but she would find out who'd killed them. They hadn't deserved to be murdered in cold blood.

MADDOX SENSED ROSE was on the verge of falling apart. Hell, at this point, who could blame her?

Two days ago, she'd been engaged, planning her wedding, and looking forward to the future.

Not only was she scared for her life now, but she'd also lost the only family she'd ever known.

Worse, they'd died a violent death.

And the questions surrounding their murder and the attempt on her life roused suspicions that her parents weren't who they said they were.

That they'd lied to Rose.

Rose followed him outside, and he unlocked the car, opened the driver's door and checked inside. The vehicle appeared to be empty.

Maddox looked over his shoulder at Rose, who was peering in the backseat of the car.

"Did your parents always keep the car this clean?"

"Yes. My father was a fanatic. He wiped it down every night."

Maddox's suspicions kicked in again as the strong scent of chemicals wafted from the interior. "He cleaned with bleach?"

"Sometimes. I told you he was obsessive."

Maddox searched the glove compartment and found a bill of sale and proof of insurance in Syd Worthington's name. A pack of gum was inside, but again no cell phone. He hadn't found a checkbook, accounting book, or any financial records in the house, so he searched for them in the car, but found nothing.

He popped the trunk and found two overnight bags tucked neatly inside.

"That's their bags," Rose said.

"The fact that they're in the car instead of the closet means they must have been planning to leave before they were killed."

Rose flinched. "You think they knew someone was after them?"

"It's beginning to look that way." He sighed. "They might have known you were in danger, too."

"Oh, God," Rose said in a haunted whisper. "They called the store two days ago, out of the blue. I was surprised and confused. They hadn't called in months."

"Did they leave a message?"

"No." Rose shivered "I was making plans to elope with Thad, and I knew if I told them, they'd try to talk me out of it. So I...didn't call them back."

Maddox grimaced. *Had they been calling to warn her that she was in danger?*

Chapter Eleven

Maddox thought of his own father dying at home and understood the pain Rose must be feeling. Except he and his father had gotten along, whereas she and her mother and father had been estranged.

Like he and his brothers. One reason he needed to rectify the situation. He could see the regrets in Rose's eyes. He didn't want those where his family was concerned.

Complicating matters more, the questions were obviously hitting her, raising doubts about everything she'd known about her parents and upbringing.

Maddox considered waiting on the crime team, but he wanted answers fast. Rose's life might depend on it. He'd share anything he found with them.

He photographed the suitcases, then hauled them from the trunk to examine them, hoping to find something inside to offer a clue as to where the couple intended to go.

Rose leaned against the car while he removed the larger bag and opened it. Women's slacks and blouses, underwear, a pair of boots and another pair of walking shoes, three colorful scarves, a toiletry bag containing basic supplies along with several pairs of contact lenses, and a small cosmetic case with powder, lip gloss and a comb.

The number of contact lens boxes struck him as odd.

"They're different colored contacts," he said to Rose. "They were altering their eye color."

"Why would they do that?"

"To disguise themselves."

Rose stared at him in disbelief. "I can't believe this is happening. I feel like I don't even know them now."

He searched the outer zipper pockets, but found nothing. No itinerary, plane, bus or train tickets, no checkbook or cash.

He opened the second bag. Men's pants and shirts lay inside, neatly folded. A shaving kit, a pair of boots, a rain jacket and three different work uniforms—with three different labels. One was from a construction company, another read Talberts' Heating and Air and the third said Germaine's Delivery Service. There were also two baseball hats.

"Have you seen these uniforms before?" Maddox asked.

Rose shook her head. "No, as far as I know, Dad never worked for any of those companies."

Maddox dug deeper, discovered a fake bottom and removed a manila envelope. He laid it on top of the clothes and removed the contents.

Several thousand dollars in cash, along with fake driver's licenses and two passports. All under the names Jeannie and Hal Kern.

Rose gasped at the sight of the cash. "Where did that come from? My parents never had any money to speak of."

"Maybe they'd been saving," Maddox said. "I don't see a checkbook or savings account book in here and I didn't find one in the house."

"They didn't trust banks," Rose said. "But Dad made a meager living, not enough to save that kind of cash."

He showed her the ID. "Do you recognize these names?"

"No." She looked up at Maddox with pain-filled eyes. "They were aliases, weren't they? My parents were afraid someone was after them, and they had money and fake IDs and planned to run."

"It appears that way," Maddox said. "I'll have CSI search the house more thoroughly. If they had this kind of money, chances are they might have more hidden in the house."

"They were killed because of me," Rose said, her voice cracking.

Maddox stepped toward her and cupped her face between his hands. "They were killed because of secrets they were keeping," Maddox said. "Because they weren't who they said they were."

Of course, Rose was part of that secret. He just didn't know if they'd been protecting her from something, or someone, or if they'd kidnapped her from her birth family and had died trying to protect themselves from being caught.

ROSE STUDIED THE NAMES on the driver's licenses as the CSI team arrived and went to work.

Jeannie and Hal Kern. She'd never heard of them.

"I wonder if they were going to tell me they were leaving, if that's the reason they called." Maybe they'd finally decided to confess the truth—whatever that was.

"Hopefully the lab can tell us their real identities."

Rose sighed. "If Worthington was a fake name, then Rose Worthington isn't my real name, either."

Maddox squeezed her arm. "I don't know, Rose, but I won't stop until I find the answer for you." He searched her face. "Can you think of anyone that your parents would confide in?"

She shook her head. "Like I said before, they kept to themselves and didn't have close friends."

"How about when you were small?"

Rose rubbed her forehead, a headache threatening. "No, but I don't remember much before we lived in Tulsa."

"You lived in Oklahoma?"

She nodded. "When I was in grade school. And some man did come by then, but I don't remember his name. My father took him into the study and closed the door so they could talk."

"You don't know what they talked about?"

"No, but right after that, we packed up and moved to Texas."

"How long did you live there?"

"About four years. One day I got home from high school, and they had the car loaded. They said my dad's job had changed and we left." She remembered her frustration. She'd just signed up to work on the yearbook and had been excited because a cute guy named Sam had been the editor.

"Is that when you moved to Wyoming?"

"Yes."

"I want to talk to the people your father worked with." He led the way to speak to the CSI team.

Rose glanced at the living room, her heart aching at the sight of the investigators tearing apart the house.

"If there's any evidence here, it's well hidden," the CSI who'd introduced himself as Hoberman said. "Either that, or the killer searched the place first and took anything incriminating with him." He frowned at Maddox. "Did you take anything?"

Maddox cursed. "No. I'm the sheriff and I want answers. We can get those better if we all work together."

The music box on the mantel drew her gaze, and she glanced at the collection in the curio cabinet. Her mother had loved music boxes—it was her one decadent pleasure, she'd said. Whenever they traveled, she'd scour antiques shops and garage and estate sales in search of new ones. Her mother had listened intently to the origin and history behind each piece, had thought them romantic.

Those trips had been special to Rose and had piqued her interest in antiques.

Maddox handed the fake IDs to Hoberman. "I found these in the suitcases in the car. Let me know what you find on them."

Rose cleared her throat. "Is it all right if I take my mother's music box collection with me? They…were special to her."

Maddox glanced at Hoberman. "You've dusted them for prints?"

Hoberman nodded. "Yes. I don't see any reason you can't have them, Miss Worthington," Hoberman said. "But this is a crime scene, so don't take anything else."

Rose agreed, although there was nothing else in the house she wanted.

"Did your mother keep a journal?" Hoberman asked.

"No, not that I know of."

A memory tickled Rose's mind. *Her parents shredding mail.* Once they paid a bill, they destroyed the paperwork. They'd never allowed her to write old classmates once they'd moved, either.

God…she'd been so frustrated with them for cutting her off from making friends.

Now she realized everything about their life had been secretive. Planned. Orchestrated to keep anyone from knowing who they really were.

MADDOX'S PHONE BUZZED just as he was getting ready to leave the Worthingtons' house. His heart stopped for a moment at the sight of his home number.

He prayed his father hadn't taken a turn for the worse.

"Excuse me, I have to get this," he said to Hoberman. "I'll check back with you about the lab results and the autopsy. See if the ME can get some DNA and let's run it."

Rose was holding one of the music boxes, sorrow darkening her eyes as she studied it. His phone had stopped ringing, but he didn't bother to listen to the voice mail. He called home immediately.

"Maddox," Mama Mary said.

"What's wrong? Is Dad okay?"

"His condition hasn't changed, but he's asked a dozen times today if you've talked to your brothers."

Frustration balled in Maddox's belly. "I called and explained the circumstances, Mama Mary."

"Brett and Ray have to see your father before he passes," Mama Mary said. "He needs to make peace with them."

"I know. Listen, I'm in Cheyenne, but I'll stop by later, okay?"

"Good. Yes, thank you, Maddox. You're a good son."

Maddox didn't know what to say. Brett wasn't bad. He was simply spoiled by his good looks and charm and lived in his own carefree world. Ray was another deal altogether. He had no idea what his youngest brother had been up to the past few years.

Mama Mary said goodbye, and Maddox went back inside to tell Rose he needed to leave. She had set three of the music boxes on the side table and was holding a fourth, a small egg-shaped one painted in pastels.

"Let me grab a box from my trunk and you can put them inside it."

She offered him a smile, although grief lined her eyes. He hurried to his car, grabbed a box from the trunk and returned to help her pack them up. Maddox didn't understand her attachment to the antiques, but each music box seemed to hold a memory for her.

"Mom and I got this one at a little shop in Phoenix," she said. "I begged her for it because it played music from *Mary Poppins*."

She wiped at a tear as she set it in the box with the

others. When she finished, Maddox carried them to the car and carefully placed the box in the trunk.

"I know you want to get home, Rose," Maddox said. "But I need to stop by the ranch first."

"Is something wrong?"

He drove from the house onto the highway, debating how to smooth things over with his father. He couldn't lie to him.

Maybe he'd call his brothers again…

"Maddox?"

"Sorry. That was our housekeeper. My father is ill and not doing well."

Rose murmured that she was sorry. "I shouldn't be taking you away from him right now."

The despair in her voice tore at him. "Don't apologize, Rose. I'm the sheriff. It's my job to protect the people in Pistol Whip."

She lapsed into silence again, lost in her grief as he covered the land between Cheyenne and the small town, then maneuvered the road to Horseshoe Creek.

Sympathy welled in Maddox's throat. She would have to plan a funeral as soon as the ME released the bodies.

Unfortunately he'd be doing the same thing soon.

Thankfully there were no surprises lurking in the dark to torment him when his father passed.

ROSE ALLOWED THE bittersweet memories to flow back as Maddox drove. Night had long fallen, blurring the images of the wilderness and scrub brush, the moon barely a sliver shining on the rugged land.

Trips to antique stores and garage sales had been the best memories she'd shared with her mother. It was almost as if her mother connected to the lost pieces of art and furniture, even dishes, that others had discarded or that wound up being left behind when someone died.

When she was little, Rose used to hunt through the old shops for dolls and jewelry. Sometimes she'd find bunches of costume beads and bracelets, even ear bobs, as her mother called them, in dresser drawers. And since they weren't valuable, she'd allowed Rose to carry them home to play dress-up.

She'd also found vintage dresses, including prom dresses and wedding gowns that were too worn or tattered to sell, and she'd added them to her dress-up box.

Her mother had snapped photos of her playing, but for some reason, Rose had never seen them on display.

"Did they find any photo albums tonight at the house?" Rose asked.

"No. I thought it was odd that there weren't any family pictures on the walls or the bookshelf."

"Mother and Daddy never displayed them," she said quietly. "But I vaguely remember that they did take pictures at holidays."

"Maybe they had a safety deposit box where they kept them along with other important documents. I'll ask Hoberman if his team found a key or anything referencing it or a bank. I'll also follow up with the people your father worked with tomorrow."

Maddox turned down a long graveled road, and she looked at the pastureland, cattle and horses in the distance. It was beautiful.

"Is this where you grew up?" Rose asked.

"Yeah. Horseshoe Creek has been in the family for generations. When Dad is gone, I'll keep running it."

"Didn't you say you had brothers?"

"Yeah. Brett is two years younger than me, and Ray two years younger than him. Brett is the charmer, a rodeo star. Ray…he and my dad didn't get along. Don't ask me why, but they're like oil and water."

"Are they coming back to see him now?"

"I called," Maddox said, his voice deep, raw with pain. "I don't know if they'll show up or not."

"Tell them they should settle things before it's too late."

Like it was for her and her family.

That was one regret she'd have to live with for the rest of her life.

"THE WORTHINGTONS ARE DEAD."

"Did you clean up?"

"Didn't have to. No signs of their former life anywhere in that damn house. If I hadn't done my research, I wouldn't have known it was them myself."

"What about the daughter?"

"She's still on the loose, but so far I don't think she has a clue as to what's going on. That damn sheriff of Pistol Whip is attached to her hip, though."

"Figure out a way to get rid of him."

"Won't killing a sheriff draw too much attention?"

"Then you think of something. And do it fast, before they find out the truth. If I'm exposed, so are you."

Chapter Twelve

Maddox had always been proud of his ranch, but tonight his heart felt heavy, his mind torn in different directions. Although his father wasn't gone yet, grief for his illness swelled inside him along with anger at his brothers for not being around.

"This is beautiful land," Rose said, her eyes widening as he led her up the steps to the wraparound porch.

Pride filled him. The hundred-year-old farmhouse still stood as honorable and welcoming as ever. Over the years, it had aged, and the kitchen needed updating, but it was home.

Mama Mary met him at the door, a curious look on her round face as she spotted Rose. "Maddox, thanks for coming home tonight."

"I can't stay," he said, "but I'll visit with Dad for a while." He gestured toward Rose and introduced her.

"You two want some supper?" Mama Mary asked.

"No thanks, Mama Mary, we already ate." He gave the older woman a quick peck on the cheek, and she blushed. "But maybe we'll have coffee."

"Of course. And I've got pie, your favorite. Coconut cream."

"That sounds great." Maddox looked at Rose. "Rose, let Mama Mary show you to the kitchen. I'll be down after I talk to Dad."

Rose nodded and followed Mama Mary, who was already treating Rose like she was an old friend. He'd missed his own mother terribly when she'd died, but Mama Mary had held him in her big loving arms while he'd cried. She'd been there for him and his father day and night since.

Brett adored her, and Ray grumbled, but she knew how to mellow his sour moods better than anyone.

He adjusted his hat as he climbed the steps, mentally bracing himself for seeing his father's weakened state.

It hurt every damn time he saw him.

He knocked gently, then eased open the door. His father lay against a mound of pillows, his face thin, his skin pale in the dim light. "Dad?"

"Come on in." His father waved a hand that had once been strong and dexterous, but now looked frail and age spotted beyond his years.

Maddox shut the door behind him, and walked toward the bed. "Mama Mary said you ate some soup."

"That woman is determined to fatten me up." His laugh sounded weak, but he was trying to act strong. "She said you didn't come home last night, that you were working. What's going on?"

Maddox straddled the wood chair and faced his father. Joe McCullen had always been interested in the goings-on in Pistol Whip and had been Maddox's biggest supporter when he'd run for sheriff.

"The woman who owns the antiques shop in town, Rose Worthington, was attacked by her fiancé."

"A domestic dispute?"

"Not hardly." Maddox explained about Thoreau's phone call, the photograph of the child on the milk carton and Rose's parents' murder.

His father sat up straighter. "So someone wants to kill this woman, but you don't know the reason?"

"That sums it up," Maddox said. "Although it's beginning to look like the Worthingtons were either in WITSEC or that they kidnapped Rose."

His father tugged at the sheet, folding it down neatly. "Really?"

"That's the way it's looking. Rose said they moved around a lot, that her parents always kept a suitcase ready in case they needed to leave. There was no paper trail in the house, no bank accounts, no personal photos."

"That does sound suspicious."

"I also found fake identification in their luggage, which was packed in the car. And they were shot point-blank in the head at close range."

"A professional hit?"

"It appears that way."

His father coughed, a ragged sound that tore at Maddox's heart. "It sounds like you need to take care of her," his father said. "That woman needs you in her corner."

Maddox's voice cracked. "I want to be here for you, too, Dad."

An awkward silence stretched between them, filled with the depressing reality of his father's illness. "Did you talk to your brothers?"

"I called and left a message for Brett but haven't heard back yet. I'll try him again tonight."

A sad look passed over his father's face. "And Ray?"

Ray's words echoed in Maddox's head—Ray was going to think about it. But he didn't want to tell his father about the conversation. "Don't worry. He'll come. I'll see to it."

His father lifted his head and studied him for a long moment. "You are an honorable man, son. I'm proud of you."

Maddox stuffed his hands in his pockets when what he wanted to do was cry like a baby.

"Now, enough coddling your old man. Go take care of Rose. She needs you now more than I do."

"Dad—"

"It's all right, Maddox. It's time you found someone special in your life, you know."

"Dad," Maddox said, his voice tight. "Rose is just a… case. Business."

A tiny smile tugged at the corners of his father's mouth. "Damn. I was hoping there was more to it. It'd be nice to know there were more McCullens coming along to keep up the family legacy."

ROSE STUDIED THE big old-fashioned kitchen with the red-checkered tablecloth and curtains, and felt like she'd stepped back in time to a place where families gathered for a big breakfast, to talk and linger over huckleberry pie and hot coffee. No texting or phones at the table, just sharing conversation.

"You look plumb worn out, child," the chubby woman said with a sympathetic smile. "Sit down and let Mama Mary take care of you."

Exhausted, Rose sank into the oak chair at the table. She wanted to lay her head down, close her eyes and forget the past two days.

She wanted to cry her heart out.

But she was too numb to do anything but sit and let the older woman fill a mug with hot coffee, then slide a piece of coconut cream pie toward her.

"Milk or sugar for your coffee, hon?" Mama Mary asked.

"Sugar, please," Rose said, tears clogging her throat at the woman's kindness. "Thank you."

Mama Mary waved her dishrag at Rose as if to say it was nothing. "I like taking care of this family. When poor Miss Grace died, Mr. Joe and the boys needed someone."

She gestured toward a framed photograph of three little boys on the wall by the table. "Maddox was ten, but he grew up real fast after that. He became serious, responsible—the caretaker."

Rose's chest squeezed as she imagined Maddox grieving yet taking care of his little brothers at the same time. "I'm sure the boys and Mr. McCullen were grateful for you."

"That works both ways. I was alone, too, lost my own husband to cancer a few years back. The McCullens believe in family and gave me a home."

"I'm so sorry for your loss, but it sounds like the arrangement was good for everyone."

"It was." Mama Mary gestured toward the pie. "Now eat up, honey."

Rose scooped up a spoonful of the dessert and swallowed it. "This is delicious."

"It's not fancy by any means. But it's Mr. Joe and Maddox's favorite."

"I'm sorry to hear he's ill," Rose said softly.

Mama Mary dabbed at her eyes. "He's a good man. I know Maddox acts tough, but he's hurtin' inside. Them two is close."

Rose nodded, her heart aching for Maddox.

"Maddox told me you got troubles of your own." Mama Mary sighed. "But you can trust him to take care of you, Rose. He's loyal to a fault. And when he says something, he means it."

Worry knitted Mama Mary's brows. "Now those other two boys, they're good, too, but they ain't been around much. They were all lost for a while. I guess everyone grieves in their own way." She folded a dishcloth as she talked, as if she needed to keep her hands busy. "Brett acts like he's fun-loving and a jokester, but that boy's got a tender side. And Ray…that young'un let his grief turn to anger. Being the baby, he was always closer to his mama than his daddy." She patted the cloth in her lap. "Sorry I'm rambling on about family."

"It's all right," Rose said softly. "I understand. I lost my own parents."

Mama Mary squeezed Rose's hands. "I am truly sorry, Rose. Maybe you came into Maddox's life for a reason. You two can understand each other."

"Maybe." Rose stared down into the coffee, willing herself to be strong. Maybe if she'd had brothers or sisters, she wouldn't feel so alone. Another reason Maddox should repair his relationship with his siblings.

Footsteps sounded, and he appeared at the door, his big body filling the space with his masculine presence.

"Sit down and eat up." Mama Mary took his arm and guided him to the table. "I'll get you a slice of pie. You look like you're on your last leg."

"I'm fine, Mama Mary," Maddox said. "But thanks for the dessert."

"Wish I could do more," she said, her voice warbling.

Maddox put his arm around Mama Mary. "You do more than you know," he said in a gruff tone. "You're family, Mama Mary."

Tears blurred the woman's eyes, and she batted at Maddox as if to brush off his words. But Rose recognized the affection between the two.

Even though they weren't blood-related, they obviously loved each other as if they were.

In fact, they were more of a family than she'd ever been with the man and woman who'd raised her.

MADDOX PINCHED THE bridge of his nose to stem his emotions as he released Mama Mary.

Maybe if his brothers did return, she could help convince them that they needed to make up with his father before he passed.

He took his usual seat and accepted the pie and coffee

Mama Mary set in front of him. Rose wiped her mouth on a napkin, but her hand was shaky.

"That was delicious," Rose said. "Thank you again."

"I can pack you up some to take with you." Without waiting on a response, Mama Mary pulled a plastic container from the cabinet and set two pieces of pie inside.

Maddox gave her a smile. "You're the best, Mama Mary. I'm going to drive Rose home now. She's had a long day." And tomorrow would be long as well.

"Will you be home later, Maddox?"

He shook his head. "No, not unless you need me."

She patted his shoulder. "Just be careful."

Maddox heard the concern in her voice, and gave her another hug. "Don't worry about me. Just take care of Dad and call me if his condition changes."

She nodded, then gave Rose a hug. "Honey, take care and come back."

Rose thanked her again, and Maddox led the way outside.

"She's wonderful," Rose said as they descended the porch steps and walked to his car.

"Yeah, she is." His father's comment about settling down struck Maddox as Rose's soulful eyes met his. In the dim moonlight with the rugged land of Horseshoe Creek behind her, she looked so beautiful that his chest clenched.

Beautiful and vulnerable, and small, fragile, as if one of Wyoming's gusty winds could literally blow her over.

He inhaled the fresh night air, breathing deeply of his heritage and the home his father had kept here for him and his brothers, of his grandfather, who'd passed it down to his father, and his grandfather's father, who'd built it years ago.

He knew his lineage, where he'd come from, had the security of knowing his parents had loved him and loved each other.

Nothing could take that away from him.

But Rose's past was a mystery to her.

Worse, when they found the answers they were looking for, she might not like them. He just hoped the truth didn't destroy her.

ROSE COULDN'T HELP but compare Maddox's farmhouse to her own parade of houses. His was a home. Hers had been mere places to live for short periods. As they left, she'd noted the wall of pictures of the boys growing up: the horseback rides across the ranch, the brothers fishing and wading in the creek, a cattle drive where they'd roasted hot dogs over a campfire.

Even the house she rented now seemed impersonal. She'd rented instead of bought, mentally planning not to stay too long from as early on as the day she'd moved in. Old habits…

She'd followed her mother's example, leaving the walls bare and the decorations to a minimum. No family pictures, no homemade Afghans like the crocheted one she'd spotted over the chair in the den, no pies or cakes in the oven.

Everything was neat and orderly. Contained. Perfect. Everything in its place.

Only beneath that perfect order lay secrets that had gotten her parents killed and brought a murderer after her.

Maddox's cell phone buzzed, and he snatched it up and answered it. "Yeah." A long pause. "Okay. Thanks for the information."

Rose tensed as he ended the call. "What is it?"

"That was a US Marshal named Lou Baxter. He claims he may know the identities of the remains we found at that cabin."

Rose's breath caught. "How did he know about them?"

"Apparently when the crime team put the information about them into the database to search for their identities, it caught the attention of the Marshals Service. Baxter is coming to Pistol Whip tomorrow and wants to meet."

Nerves tingled along her spine.

Finding out the identity of the dead people on that land might lead them to Thad's real identity and to her parents' killer.

Chapter Thirteen

Rose stowed the pie Mama Mary had packed for her in the refrigerator while Maddox carried the assortment of music boxes inside. But that phone call disturbed him. Marshal Baxter had insisted on meeting him the next morning.

Alone.

Which meant that he had bad news—or that the man might not trust Rose.

Did she know more than she was telling him?

Her shoulders slumped with fatigue as she carefully placed each music box on the mantel with the one she already owned.

"Do you remember the story behind each one of those?"

"Some of them, but not all," Rose said. "I never quite understood why my mother loved them so much, but she never bought anything for herself so my father didn't complain." She ran her finger along the gold trim of a hand-painted carousel-shaped music box. "She was particularly intrigued by the years they were made."

"Interesting." Although he didn't know the significance. "Did they ever mention the name Baxter to you?"

A sliver of fear darted across Rose's face. "No, not that I remember."

She traced a finger over the scar again, her brows furrowed.

The cuckoo clock in the hall chirped that it was midnight, drawing Rose's gaze to it.

Tears blurred her eyes, and she turned away. "I'm going to bed. If you need to go home and stay with your father tonight, please do so, Maddox. I feel guilty taking you away from him when he's ill."

The fact that she was trying to be strong stirred his admiration. No woman who was selfless enough to tell him to leave when she was scared for her life could be lying.

She was in pain but she still had enough compassion to worry about him.

A seed of longing sprouted inside him. He wanted to touch her, hold her, comfort her. Assuage her pain.

Unable to help himself, he took a step toward her, but she turned away. His breath hitched at the sight of her shoulders shaking with the tears she tried to hide.

"Don't worry about me and don't feel guilty. I want to be here for you."

Rose sniffed. "I'll never see them again," she said in a ragged whisper. "Never get to tell them I'm sorry, that I loved them." A sob escaped her. "Never get to ask them why they lied to me."

"I know, I'm sorry." He wanted to reach for her but fisted his hands by his side. "But we will find out who you are and what happened years ago, Rose. I swear."

She dropped her face into her hands, breaking his heart, and he gently took her by the arms and turned her to face him. With his thumb, he lifted her chin and looked into her eyes, disturbed by the pain and sorrow reflected in the depths. "I promise, Rose. I know you're hurting now, and confused about why they kept things from you, but if they aren't your birth parents, they must have cared for you or they wouldn't have raised you."

She gave a tiny nod, although a mixture of anger and denial darkened her face.

"They also moved around to protect you."

"Did they?" Rose asked. "Or were they moving around to keep my real family from finding me?"

ROSE CHOKED ON the words. The myriad of emotions swirling in her head made her dizzy.

"I don't know, Rose, but try not to dwell on it tonight." Maddox stroked her hair back from her cheek and brushed at a tear. "Just get some rest."

She dropped her head against his chest on a sigh. "I don't even know how to feel, Maddox. I'm so confused."

"I know," he murmured as he folded his arms around her.

Rose leaned into him, her breathing steadying as she relaxed against him. They stood there for a long time, him silently comforting her, her taking solace in his solid body and quiet strength.

Thad had been showy and charming and said all the right things.

But he'd been a liar and a con man.

Maddox was the opposite. He didn't try to impress with fancy words. But a rock-steady confidence radiated from him that made her crave more of his presence.

And his touch.

He stroked her hair gently, soothing her with whispered murmurings, and heat replaced the coldness that had swallowed her when she'd stepped into her parents' home and found them dead.

The past two days had been filled with horrors she'd never imagined. Just for a moment, she wanted to forget the reality that faced her. The funeral plans, the questions, the loss…the danger.

Her heart thumped wildly as she lifted her head and searched Maddox's face. He was being kind to her, doing his job, but did he feel the jolt of awareness that zinged through her when his gaze met hers?

Rose had never felt so alone.

Yet Maddox had a way of erasing that loneliness with his tenderness.

Aching for more, she lifted one hand and pressed it to his cheek. His jaw clenched, his breath hissing out between his teeth. The wide mouth that had been set in a grim line most of the day settled into a sensual smile that turned her inside out.

"Rose—"

"Shh." She pressed one finger to his mouth, then stood on tiptoe and closed her lips to his. One touch, and her heart fluttered with longing for another.

She threaded her fingers into his hair and pulled him closer, moving her mouth against his until he gave in with a low groan and kissed her back.

His hand moved along her hip to hold her more intimately against him as his tongue teased her lips apart. Rose succumbed to the hunger driving her and savored the taste of him as he deepened the kiss.

His hand stroked her hip and his sex hardened against her stomach. The heat emanating from his body to hers ignited a flame inside her stronger than anything she'd ever felt with Thad.

Thad...dear God, what was she doing? Throwing herself at Maddox when he knew she'd already been a fool for another man?

Self-disgust shot through her, and she wrenched herself away. "I'm sorry, Maddox, I...shouldn't have done that."

He stiffened, his hands dropping to his sides. "It was my fault. I...shouldn't have touched you."

He was letting her off the hook when they both knew that she'd initiated the kiss. Heck, she'd practically begged him for it.

"It's been a long day, Rose. Go to bed."

This time his voice sounded gruff, his words almost an order.

She glanced down and saw the bulge in his jeans and realized he needed distance between them. After all, he was a man and she had rubbed herself against him.

His reaction was normal. A physical reaction. It certainly didn't mean that he wanted her personally.

So she turned and hurried up the steps to her bedroom, willing herself to keep the tears from falling until she closed the bedroom door and collapsed on the bed alone.

DAMMIT. MADDOX STRODE outside onto Rose's porch and cursed himself for losing his head.

But the sadness in Rose's eyes and the anguish in her voice had nearly undone him. Coupled with his own emotions over his father's illness, his frustration with his brothers and his anxiety over this investigation, he'd found it damn hard to walk away.

Still, he was a lawman, prided himself on maintaining control, on compartmentalizing and remaining professional.

But no woman had ever touched him like Rose. Not just physically, but on another level. She made him want to be a better man, to slay her dragons and make her smile, and promise her things that he had no right to promise her.

A noise sounded from the woods, and he surveyed the property, his instincts kicking in. Someone had tried to kill Rose once, and they might make another attempt.

Her life depended on him remaining alert and being prepared for another attack.

He rubbed his hand over his gun, then jogged down the porch steps and walked around the edge of the house, scanning the backyard and woods for anything suspicious. The back door was locked. Windows closed.

Nothing stood out.

So why did he feel as if someone was watching Rose now, waiting to strike?

Night noises echoed from the land beyond, and a coyote howled somewhere nearby.

Finally he grew weary and went back in the house. It was quiet upstairs. Hopefully Rose had fallen asleep. God knew she'd been through hell, and had to be wiped out.

The call from the marshal echoed in his head, and that uneasy feeling hit him again. Was he anxious about what the man had to say?

Or because he should have already called the Marshals Service himself?

Sweat beaded his neck, and he filled a glass with water and chugged it, then punched the number for the marshal's office in Cheyenne. Maybe Baxter would give him a hint as to what he had to tell him.

But a voice mail clicked on, so he left a message asking Baxter to call him.

If he knew what he was dealing with, maybe he could warn Rose in the morning before he met with the man.

Rose ducked into the closet and hid behind the coats. Her mommy was screaming and crying. Then she yelled for her to run and hide and not to come out.

Outside the room, a tree branch beat against the house. Rain pounded the roof. Another noise made her jump.

She was shaking so hard her knees knocked together. What was happening? Who was that bad man at the door? Why did he have a gun?

Why were Mommy and Daddy so upset?

She didn't like it here in the dark. Something cold touched her foot. A snake? Spider? Roach?

She shook her legs and feet, then grabbed a coat to wrap around her to keep the icky bugs off. The coat smelled funny, like dirty socks and dust and something else stinky, like that brown stuff Daddy drank sometimes.

Another noise made her jump. Then more shouting, and a popping sound so loud that she thought the roof was going to explode.

Rose buried her face in her hands to keep from crying. Daddy said to be quiet. Hide and don't make a sound. Don't let anyone know you're in the house.

Another popping sound and Mommy screamed again. Then a big clunk like someone fell. More noises. Shoes pounding the floor.

Furniture being moved. A lamp or something glass broke. Doors opened and slammed shut.

Was the bad man leaving?

Another boom like something heavy fell on the floor. Mommy's crying got quiet. Daddy yelled something, but his voice sounded funny. Far away.

Lights flickered on. Footsteps clattered. Someone was coming toward the closet.

She balled herself up as little as she could and covered her head with the coat. Dust filled her nose and mouth, but she shoved her face down hard and bit her lip to keep from crying.

What would the bad man do if he found her?

She didn't know how long she stayed there, but she closed her eyes and tried to think about Christmas and the dollhouse she wanted Santa to bring, and how fun it would be to make sugar cookies with Mommy. But tears blurred her eyes and she kept hearing sounds and the rain got louder.

She didn't know how long she hid in there, but she thought it got quiet and maybe the bad man was gone.

She inched up on her knees and peered through the crack in the door.

Then she saw the man. He yanked her mommy by the hair. Then he shoved a gun at her face.

The gun went boom and then all Rose saw was red...

ROSE JERKED AWAKE, shaking and sweating. She couldn't breathe.

Tears streamed down her face as she stumbled from bed and fought for air. Suddenly the door burst open, and a man's big shadow filled the doorway.

Rose screamed, the red blinding her.

Then the man reached for her. She beat at his hands, fighting to get away, but his arms closed around her, holding her so tightly that she couldn't move.

"Rose, it's me, Maddox," a deep voice said. "Stop fighting, you're safe."

His words finally registered through the haze of her panic, and she blinked to clear her vision. But the red blended with the darkness, and she couldn't make out Maddox's face.

"You were having a nightmare," Maddox murmured against her ear. "But you're safe now. I'm here."

She closed her eyes and collapsed against him. *It was a nightmare, wasn't it?*

Or...had it been real, a memory, not a dream?

Chapter Fourteen

Maddox's heart had seized the moment he heard Rose's scream.

He'd imagined the man who'd attacked her sneaking in and trying to kill her again, so he'd barreled up the steps, gun drawn.

He held her until her shaking subsided, then leaned back against the headboard and pulled her up next to him. She lay her head on his chest and curled up beside him, and he curved his arm around her shoulder, determined to make her feel safe.

Yet her eyes still looked glazed.

"What happened in the dream?" he asked softly.

Her breath hitched. "I was a little girl, four or five years old. And my parents were home, but someone else was there, someone they were afraid of."

Maddox tensed. "You're talking about the Worthingtons?"

She shook her head. "I don't think so. I think it might have been before they took me. When I lived with my birth parents."

So she did think the Worthingtons had taken her? "What happened?"

"Someone came in the house, and my mother told me to hide. I darted in the closet and crawled behind the coats. It

was dark and my dad was shouting, and my mother screaming, then it sounded like they were fighting with someone,
a man, turning over furniture."

Maddox rubbed her shoulder with his thumb, hoping to
keep her calm. "Go on."

Rose sniffled. "I was terrified but I peeked through the
crack in the door and…" Her fingers dug into his chest,
her agitation escalating. "A man shot my mother, and then
there was red everywhere…blood…so much of it. That's
all I could see…blood…"

He wrapped his arms around her again, soothing her.
"It was just a dream, Rose."

She shook her head against him, then looked up at him,
her face haunted. "It seemed so real, though, like it happened…like I was there."

Maddox considered her comment. If she had witnessed
her parents' murder, then she might have been placed in
foster care or been given to a relative afterward. If the
Worthingtons took custody of her, they might have gone
into WITSEC to protect her.

It would explain a lot.

"Have you had other memories similar to this?"

"No." She clamped her teeth over her lower lip for a moment as if she had to think about the question. "Although
the night Thad attacked me, when that gun went off, for
a second, everything went blank. Well, not blank, but an
image of blood flashed behind my eyes."

"From a gunshot wound?"

She nodded. "Blood spraying on the floor…"

He tilted her face up to study her. "Rose, you said you
saw a man standing over your mother, that he shot her."

"Yes." Her voice cracked.

"Did you see his face?"

Rose closed her eyes and pressed her palms against them
as if trying to visualize the shooter. "No, it was dark and

he…had his back to me. He yanked my mother up by the hair and pressed the gun to her temple and…*God…*" She choked on the words. "He shot her."

Maddox gritted his teeth. If Rose had witnessed her birth mother's murder, the killer was probably afraid her memory would return and she'd send him to prison.

But it had been twenty years. Why come after her now?

By the time daylight dawned, Rose forced herself to crawl from bed—and Maddox's arms.

He had been nothing but chivalrous when he'd consoled her.

Although she'd wanted more…

She climbed in the shower while he brewed coffee and changed in the downstairs bathroom. Apparently he kept a duffel bag with extra clothes in his trunk for emergencies when he worked a case all night.

But as she dressed, the memory of that nightmare taunted her with the fact that it might have actually happened. That she'd had another set of parents who'd been murdered in their home when she was little.

Had she seen the man's face, and been too traumatized to remember it? Or had his face remained hidden in the shadows?

She dried her hair and applied powder to camouflage the dark circles beneath her eyes. The lack of sleep and worry showed in the shadows and lines on her face.

What did Maddox see when he looked at her? A foolish woman who'd fallen for a con man who'd lied to her?

Irritated with herself for caring what he thought, she brushed her unruly hair and pulled it back at the nape of her neck with a silver clasp. By the time she entered the kitchen, Maddox was sipping coffee and had two plates of eggs on the table along with toast.

"Thank you for making this," she said, although her stomach was still tied in knots.

He gestured for her to sit and handed her a mug of coffee, then he wolfed down his food. "I have to meet that marshal this morning. Then I want to check in with the ME and Hoberman."

"I'll go with you to meet the marshal," Rose said.

Maddox's jaw tightened. "I want to speak to him alone first."

"Why?"

Maddox carried his empty plate to the dishwasher, rinsed it and placed it inside. "Because you've been through enough, Rose. Let me take you some place safe, then I'll report back after I talk to him and drop by the morgue."

"Do you think they'll release my parents' bodies today?" *Although if that dream was a memory, her actual birth parents had died twenty years ago.*

"I doubt it. The autopsy will take time, and we need to verify their identities."

Despair threatened to overwhelm her. She needed to grieve their loss, but so many questions still remained unanswered for her to know how she felt. Sad? Angry?

Alone...

Maddox folded his arms. "You can stay at my ranch while I'm gone."

"Thanks," Rose said, although she didn't want to put Mama Mary in danger. "But I should stop by Vintage Treasures today." She gestured toward the music boxes. "My mother never kept written records of the history of the boxes she collected. She always said she kept the stories in her head. But I'd like to research them so I know the history behind each one."

She also needed to start thinking about funeral arrangements for her parents. But she couldn't face that yet.

"Are you going to sell the music boxes?"

"No, they're all I have of my mom." She retrieved her cell phone to take pictures of the pieces to take with her to the store. "At least the woman I thought was my mother."

MADDOX DIDN'T KNOW how to respond so he gave her time to assimilate everything that had happened as he drove her to Vintage Treasures.

Who was Rose's birth mother?

He didn't think it was the woman who'd raised her as Rose Worthington, but he refrained from speculating. He needed to get the facts.

He studied Rose's antiques shop as she unlocked the door and they went inside. Furniture, picture frames, dishes, artwork, clothing, homemade quilts and Afghans and other assorted items filled the store. Collections of rare coins, thimbles, lace, dolls and even arrowheads were displayed near a sitting area, where Rose served tea, coffee and shortbread cookies.

The bell over the door tinkled, and a young woman with short, spiky dark hair entered, an oversized bag slung over one shoulder, her denim-and-lace dress similar to the vintage clothing on display in the far right hand corner of the shop.

The young woman looked him up and down then smiled at Rose. "Hey, Rose. I didn't think you'd be in today."

"I needed to do some research." She waved a hand toward him. "Trina, do you know the sheriff, Maddox McCullen?"

Trina gave him a flirtatious smile and extended her hand. "No. I mean I've seen you around town, Sheriff, but it's nice to finally meet. I'm Trina Fields."

Maddox shook her hand and forced a smile in return, although he kept it professional. Trina was attractive, but not his type.

Hell, he didn't have a type...

Rose. Yes, Rose was his type. Dammit.

"What's going on, Rose?" Trina asked.

"It turned out that Thad lied to me. He attacked me the other night and then disappeared." She started to confess about shooting him, but Maddox shook his head to silence her. Thankfully she understood.

"Oh, my God," Trina said. "Rose, are you okay?"

"Yes. Sheriff McCullen is looking for him." She clutched Trina's hand. "But listen, this is just between us."

"How can I help?" Trina asked.

"Just watch out for him or anyone else suspicious," Maddox said. "If you see him or hear from him, call me. And don't let him in your home or the store."

Trina threw an arm around Rose. "Don't worry, I'll take care of her. Just find the son of a bitch."

Maddox grinned at her moxie. Rose might think she was alone, but obviously Trina cared about her. And having another pair of eyes watching out for Rose couldn't hurt.

Although if Thad knew Rose cared about Trina, he might use her to get to Rose.

SHAME FILLED ROSE as Maddox left. Trina was looking at her with such pity that she hated for her coworker to know the truth.

When Trina had first come to work for her, she'd been reluctant to get close to the young woman.

Although Trina had asked a lot of questions, too— questions about where Rose came from, what inspired her to delve into the antiques business, where she'd attended school, even what her favorite foods were and if she had allergies. Just chitchat, girls getting to know each other, Trina had said.

But Rose had held back, unable to trust. Trina's questions had felt intrusive, too personal, as if Trina was looking for a best friend.

Something Rose had never had.

Uncomfortable, she'd erected her usual walls and avoided personal topics and get-togethers. No dinners or drinks after work. No morning jogs or coffee on the weekends. All business, no play.

Old habits were hard to break.

And then she'd let Thad worm his way beyond her defenses…

What a mistake.

"You want to talk about it, Rose?" Trina asked.

Rose shook her head. "Not yet. I…have to figure out some things first. But…my parents were killed yesterday, so I'll need some time off in the next week or so to make the arrangements."

Trina ran her hand through her spiked hair, fluffing her bangs, a nervous gesture Rose had noticed when she'd first met her and Trina applied for the job. "I'm so sorry. What happened?"

The words stuck in Rose's throat. *They were murdered in cold blood.* "Like I said, I'm not ready to talk about it yet. I'm still in shock."

"Then go home, Rose, take time. I can handle the customers today."

Rose looked around the store. She felt more comfortable, more at home here than anywhere else. "I really need to keep busy today," Rose said. "To take my mind off the situation for a little while. I thought I'd research some of my mother's music boxes."

"Is there anything I can do?"

Rose gave Trina a hug. "Just bear with me and be ready to fill in when I need to be gone."

Trina nodded. "Of course. Whatever you need."

Rose thanked her, then carried her phone to the computer in her office to research the music boxes, grateful Trina hadn't pushed her for more information.

How could she tell her about her past and her family when she wasn't sure she knew anything about them herself?

ANXIETY KNOTTED MADDOX's shoulders as he left Pistol Whip and drove toward the warehouse district ten miles outside of town where Baxter suggested they meet. He hadn't received a call back from the Marshals Service, but an early morning text from Baxter expressed concern about being followed. He didn't want to endanger Rose by leading a killer to her door.

The area was deserted, three vacant buildings sitting on empty lots that had been built two years ago for companies relocating to the area, moves that never happened. The town had been optimistic about another company moving into the buildings and boosting the economy, but so far no one had committed.

Senses alert, Maddox kept his eyes peeled as he turned into the vacant parking lot. He checked his watch.

Baxter was late.

His phone buzzed. Hoberman. He punched Connect.

"Thought I'd give you an update," Hoberman began. "We didn't find a safety deposit box key at the Worthingtons or any indication that the couple had stashed away stolen money. We hit a wall with the prints as well."

If the couple had been in WITSEC, the marshals would have covered their tracks and eliminated their prints from the system. "I'm meeting with a US Marshal now," Maddox said. "Maybe he can fill in the holes."

Nerves on edge, he disconnected, climbed from the car and walked across the parking lot, then decided to take a look inside the warehouse in case something had happened to Baxter.

The lock on the first warehouse had been broken, so

he eased open the door, but a sound broke the silence. A ticking…

Maddox's heart jumped to his throat. He released the door and started to run.

But the bomb exploded, metal flying and pelting him as the impact hurled him through the air to the ground.

Chapter Fifteen

Rose emailed the photos of the music boxes to her computer, then started with the first one and began a search for the origin.

The antique music box turned out to be one with a bisque doll with flowers from the nineteenth century that played Mozart.

The history of the sale showed that it had been authenticated through a reputable antiques auction house. She followed the story of how it had been passed along through two generations of families, then wound up being found in a storage bin, which eventually ended up being sold because no one had claimed the contents.

The tinkle of the bell in the front indicated a customer, then footsteps sounded. Tired from her restless night, she decided to stay put in the office and let Trina handle it. She didn't feel like having to be social today.

She plugged in the picture of the second music box, an antique portable sewing machine, and waited while her program ran its course. This one dated pre-1900s.

Trina's voice echoed from the front, then her heels clicked on the wood floor. "Yes, wait."

A man's voice came through the wall, low and ominous. Rose froze, her heart clenching.

Dear God...Thad?

No, it couldn't be.

She jumped up and peered through the door, shock immobilizing her as his face appeared in front of her.

Thad with a gun to Trina's head.

"You thought you could get away, but you thought wrong, Rose."

With one hand, he shoved Trina into the office. She stumbled and fell, crying out as her head hit the corner of the desk. Rose reached down to help her, but Thad jerked her arm and dragged her toward the back door.

MADDOX SLOWLY ROUSED from unconsciousness, his ears ringing, the world a hazy blur of smoke, crackling wood and metal. He was so disoriented he lifted his head to look around, his lungs straining for a breath. Flames shot into the sky and burning rubble was scattered everywhere.

His eyes stung, and his mind was muddled as he recalled the last moments before the explosion. He'd been waiting on Baxter to show, but the marshal was late, so he'd climbed out to look around. He'd opened the warehouse door, which was unlocked, and…boom.

The impact had sent him flying through the air, and now he was lying in the dirt, trapped.

He cursed again as reality hit him. It had been a setup.

The man who'd called and said his name was Marshal Baxter was lying about either who he was or what his intentions were. He'd asked him to come here to…

Dammit. To lure him away from Rose.

Adrenaline kicked in, and he tried to move, but his leg was pinned beneath a big piece of metal. Heat from the fire scalded his skin, the smoke acrid and thick as it curled upward through the air.

He had to get out of here. The bastard had ambushed him and now he might have Rose.

If anything happened to her, he'd never forgive himself.

No…surely she was safe. She was in town with her friend at work. Not a place where an attacker might strike.

Unless he found a way to lure her away, as he'd done to him.

Calling himself an idiot, he threw loose debris aside and rolled his upper body enough to shove at the damn metal on his leg, but it wouldn't budge. Pain ricocheted up his thigh, but he gritted his teeth and tried again. He held his breath and pushed as hard as he could, but it still didn't move.

He needed help, *dammit*.

He slid his hand down to reach inside his pocket for his cell phone, but realized he'd left it in the car. *Hell. What now?*

Heart racing, he shifted to his other elbow, searching for something to help him free himself. A long board lay less than a few feet away, pieces of it splintered and burning.

He stretched his left hand out to grab it and connected with the end. It was hot to the touch, and he nearly scalded his fingers, but he blew at them, yanked a handkerchief from his pocket and wrapped it around his hand to pad his fingers, then clawed at the board again. He missed and his fingers dug in the dirt the first time, but on the second try he snagged the plank and dragged it toward him, beating the flames in the dirt until they were extinguished.

Clenching his jaw at the pain, he shifted again, then wedged the board beneath the metal, sucked in a breath and used it to push at the metal. One, two, three tries and it finally gave an inch.

Using all the strength he possessed, he shoved it again, at the same time dragging himself forward. His effort paid off, and he managed to roll out of the way just before he lost his grip on the stick, and the metal slab fell to the ground.

Images of Thoreau or some other crazed maniac putting a gun to Rose's head and killing her in cold blood, as had been done to her parents, sent another shot of adrenaline through him, and he pushed himself up and tried to run toward the car.

His leg gave way, though, his thigh throbbing. *Hell, he didn't have time to be weak.* He snatched another board and used it like a crutch, hobbling until he reached his police car.

Wiping sweat from the back of his hand with his sleeve, he slid inside and started the engine while he punched in Rose's number.

He had to warn her that he'd walked into a trap.

But her phone rang a half dozen times, and she didn't answer. He left a voice mail, then dialed the number for the shop, but the voice mail kicked in there as well.

Pure panic fueled him, and he pressed the accelerator and roared toward town, his tires squealing.

ROSE FOUGHT TERROR at the cold look in Thad's eyes. "Thad, think about this. The sheriff knows you tried to kill me. He's looking for you."

Thad waved the gun in her face. "You made a big mistake when you shot me, Rose."

"I can't believe you survived. How?" Rose cried. "Where have you been?"

"Lying low." He rubbed at his chest. "It's a good thing I had a friend to dig out that bullet and stitch me up."

Rose glanced at Trina, her pulse pounding. Trina rolled to her back, but blood trickled down her forehead where she'd hit the table.

"Please, let's go somewhere and talk. Trina has nothing to do with this, just let her go."

Thad barked a nasty laugh. "You don't get it, Rose. Trina helped me find you."

A sense of betrayal stung Rose, and she snapped her head toward her friend. Or the young woman she'd thought was her friend.

Trina wiped at the blood on her forehead, her eyes luminous with emotions. "It wasn't like that, Rose…"

"Shut up." Thad walked over and slapped Trina across the face. "You've done your part. I don't need you anymore."

Trina cried out and pressed a hand to her cheek, tears streaming down her face. "You never said you were going to hurt her."

Shockwaves rolled through Rose. So it was true—Trina hadn't been her friend. She'd used her.

"I don't understand," Rose said, her voice warbling as she stared at Trina. "What's going on?"

"I…I'm so sorry," Trina whispered.

Rose whirled on Thad, her hands on her hips. "Why were you looking for me? What did I do to you?"

Another sinister look. "Nothing. This is just business."

"Just business?" Rose cried. "It's my life. Why do you want me dead?"

Thad shoved her backward against the door, but Rose lifted her chin. If she was going to die, she deserved to know the reason. "Who hired you, Thad?"

"You'll never know." Thad raised the gun, but suddenly Trina lurched up and jumped him from behind.

"You bastard, you lied to me." She grabbed his arm, struggling for the gun, but Thad elbowed her in the chest and aimed the weapon at her. Trina fought back though, the two of them battling for control and wrestling with the weapon.

The gun went off, and Rose screamed as Trina groaned and fell backward, blood gushing from her abdomen.

Rose raced over to her. Trina might have betrayed her, but she'd just tried to save her life.

She couldn't let her die.

MADDOX ROUNDED THE corner on two wheels, his heart hammering as he called his deputy and explained about the warehouse explosion. "I'm on my way to Rose's antiques shop. I think she's in danger. Where are you now?"

"Out at the Stanley farm on a domestic. Gave the old man a warning."

Maddox had hoped Whitefeather was in town and could get to Rose, but he was closer to town than his deputy. "Meet the crime team at the warehouse and make sure they process it thoroughly."

"Copy that," his deputy said. "I'm on my way."

Maddox scanned the parking on the street in front of the antiques shop, and noticed a dark gray sedan. His pulse jumped as he threw the police car into a parking space, jumped out and jogged to the door.

He paused to look through the front glass, but noted that the shades were drawn. The Open sign had been flipped to Closed.

The hair on the back of his neck prickled. Something was definitely wrong. If Rose was hurt, it was his fault. He'd taken the bastard's bait and walked into a trap, leaving her alone and unprotected.

He jiggled the doorknob, but it was locked. Jaw clenched, he pulled his weapon, checking to make sure no one was on the street and no children were close by.

A couple of mothers pushed their babies in strollers in the park in the center of the town. Another lady and her daughter ducked into Boot Barn, and an older couple entered the coffee shop. The general store looked busy, retirees gathering to play checkers on the whiskey barrels in front of the country store.

He inched around the side of the antiques store toward the back entrance, but just as he rounded the corner, the door opened and Rose stepped out. She looked shaken and upset, her body rigid.

Thoreau stood behind her, a .38 pressed into her back.

Maddox aimed his Colt at the man's head. "Stop, Thoreau. Let her go."

Rose's eyes widened as she met his gaze, but Thoreau yanked her in front of him to use her as a shield. "Take one step and she's dead."

Pain and fear wrenched Rose's face. "Maddox, do what he says. Trina…she needs help. She's been shot."

Maddox cursed. *Hell, Thoreau planned to kill her anyway.* But Maddox couldn't be the reason, so he played along and lifted his hands in surrender. "All right, just stay calm, Thoreau. We can work this out."

Thoreau's gaze didn't waver. "The only way this is going to work is for you to let me go."

"Then go, but leave Rose. You can get away faster without her."

Thoreau gave a firm shake of his head, an ominous harshness in his eyes. "I've come too far to stop now."

Maddox tightened his fingers around his weapon, but he didn't make a move toward Thoreau. The man's gun was way too close to Rose's back. If the SOB panicked, he might shoot her.

Thoreau shoved Rose toward a back street, where Maddox spotted a black SUV with dark tinted windows. Obviously his getaway vehicle.

"Help Trina!" Rose shouted.

Maddox stood stone-still, rage tightening every muscle in his body. Rose stumbled, and he instinctively reached out to catch her, but Thoreau gave him a warning look, and he backed away. Seconds later, Thoreau shoved Rose inside the front seat on the passenger side, then forced her to slide over to the driver's seat.

Fear for Rose vibrated in every cell of his body. He had to follow them.

But Rose wanted him to save her friend.

Anger crowded his throat as he raced inside. Trina was

lying on the floor, ashen-faced and bleeding. He stooped and felt her pulse, and she opened her eyes, although they looked weak and glassy.

"He has Rose," she said in a choked whisper.

Maddox called 911. "I know. She wanted me to save you."

A sob escaped Trina. "I'm okay, go after her. He'll kill her!"

"This is Sheriff McCullen," Maddox said to the 911 operator. "A woman has been shot at Vintage Treasures. Send an ambulance ASAP and alert the hospital that she needs surgery."

He hung up, then ran to find a cloth to press against her wound. He found some cleaning rags in the bathroom, rolled them up and pressed them to her injury.

Trina laid her hand over them as he tried to stop the bleeding. "Go, Sheriff. You have to save Rose."

Maddox was torn, but the ambulance was on its way and she was right. He rushed to his car and barreled away.

If he didn't catch Thoreau and stop him, he would lose Rose.

ROSE SWALLOWED HER TERROR as she drove from the parking lot. She needed to stay calm. Keep Thad talking... "Where are we going?"

Thad waved the gun at her. "Just drive out of town."

"Where? To some isolated place where you can kill me and leave my body like you planned to do at that cabin?"

"Yes. But you had to screw things up."

Rose couldn't believe this was the same man who'd romanced her with dinner and wine and dreams of a future together.

He gestured toward a dirt road that led west toward the mountain ridges.

Rose drove slowly, hoping to stall. Maybe Maddox

would come after her, maybe he'd find a way to save her once he got help for Trina.

Trina...why had she helped Thad?

"The least you can do is tell me why you plan to kill me," Rose said.

"I told you, it's business."

"Who hired you?"

"Stop dragging around and press the gas," Thad said as he jammed the gun against her arm. "Your buddy isn't going to find us and rescue you. It's over this time."

Panic threatened to seize Rose, but she tamped it down. "Just tell me who wants me dead and the reason. I deserve to know why I'm going to die."

"You really don't know?" Thad asked, his voice incredulous.

Rose shook her head. "All I know is that my name is Rose, you tried to kill me and then my parents turned up dead." She glared at him. "Did you kill them, too?"

"The Worthingtons weren't your parents," Thad said in a snide tone.

"They raised me," Rose said, clinging to that fact.

"They stole you," Thad said.

Rose sucked in a sharp breath. "Why would they do that?"

Thad made a low sound in his throat. "They never told you about your birth parents?"

"No."

"And you don't remember what happened when you were five?"

Irritation spiked Rose's anger. "No, why don't you fill me in."

Thad chuckled beneath his breath, a sharp sound that infuriated Rose.

"Good. If you haven't figured out what happened, then

that damn sheriff doesn't know, either. That means I have time to kill you and escape."

Rose's hands tightened around the steering wheel as rage heated her blood. The bastard wasn't going to tell her.

God help her, if she was going to die, she wouldn't go down without a fight. She'd take him with her.

She spotted a patch of trees up ahead at the bend in the road and accelerated, then swerved straight toward them as she rounded the curve.

"What the hell are you doing?" Thad tried to snatch the steering wheel, but she gripped it with all her might, gunned the engine and drove straight into the trees.

Tires screeched, glass shattered and the air bags exploded as the vehicle slammed into the massive tree trunk.

Rose's neck snapped back, pain ricocheted through her head and the world spun into oblivion.

Chapter Sixteen

Maddox flew down the road out of town, searching each side road for the SUV.

The first three streets led to neighborhoods, not a place where Thoreau would take Rose.

Too many people around.

His mind raced with ideas of where he would go, but fear clouded his thoughts. He couldn't let Rose die. He'd promised her he'd find answers, and he hadn't found them yet.

But he must be on the right track or her parents wouldn't have been murdered.

His phone buzzed, and he snatched it up. "Sheriff Mc-Cullen."

"It's Whitefeather. The crime team is combing the wreckage of the warehouse now. You have any idea who set off the bomb?"

"Yes," Maddox said. "Although I don't know the guy's real name." He explained about the attack on Rose and his investigation. "Thoreau has Rose, and I'm chasing them." Or at least he hoped he was headed in the right direction. "I called an ambulance to Vintage Treasures to take care of Rose's assistant Trina Fields. Can you follow up and let me know how she's doing at the hospital? Rose will be upset if she doesn't make it."

"I'll head over there now."

His deputy promised to call him with an update, and Maddox noticed a dirt road leading away from civilization, one that led toward the mountains past the reservation.

Fresh tire tracks marred the dirt and gravel.

Brakes squealed as he jerked the wheel to the right and barreled onto the road. He hit a pothole and cursed, but sped forward. No telling how far ahead of him Rose and Thoreau were.

He just prayed the son of a bitch hadn't hurt her.

Heart hammering double time, he searched left and right for other side roads or a place they could have pulled over to hide, but the land was barren, desolate, the sharp jutting ridges too far away for them to have made it there yet.

Images of Rose with that gun at her head made sweat bead on his skin. She'd been so understanding about his father, compassionate when she had her plate full of her own troubles.

He would not let her down.

A dark cloud rolled across the sky, casting shadows on the scrub brush and rocks ahead, but he spotted a cluster of trees just before a small ridge and saw the SUV had crashed into the thicket.

God, please don't let Rose be dead.

He accelerated, his gaze scanning the area to see if they were inside the car or outside on foot.

Thoreau could have already killed her and be dumping her body in the bushes.

Forcing that image from his mind, he drew his gun as he neared the SUV. Suddenly the driver's door opened, and Rose tumbled out. Thoreau pushed her and climbed out behind her, his face red with rage.

Maddox threw the car into Park, jumped out and ran toward them. Thoreau staggered. Rose stumbled, then collapsed onto the ground on her hands and knees.

Thoreau grabbed the back of her hair and pushed her

head down to her knees, forcing her to curl against her legs in submission. Rose screamed and tried to pull his hands from her hair, but Thoreau jammed his foot onto her back to keep her still, then pressed the gun to her head.

Maddox saw red. The bastard couldn't kill her.

Without hesitating, he raised his weapon and aimed. His lungs strained for air. If he missed, Thoreau would fire and Rose would be dead.

But if he didn't fire…she'd be dead anyway.

Forcing himself to focus, he reminded himself that he was a sharp shooter. He'd always won the skeet competitions and shooting contests, which had pissed off Brett and Ray.

A tremor in his hand threatened, but Rose cried out again, and he cursed and fired.

One bullet and he hit the bastard in the temple. Thoreau's body jerked in shock and tilted sideways, his gun skittering from his hand as he fell to the ground.

Maddox gritted his teeth, praying Rose was all right as he sprinted toward them. He kept his weapon trained on Thoreau, alert for any sign of movement.

When he reached the man, he kicked Thoreau's gun several feet away, then kneeled and checked his pulse. Nothing. His eyes were wide open in the shock of death.

Relieved the man was dead, he shoved Thoreau off Rose. She was crunched over, face down, her body still. Blood soaked the back of her blouse and hair.

Terror seized him.

Had Thoreau fired a shot before he'd died?

Maddox's breath stalled in his chest, and he leaned closer and brushed Rose's hair away from her neck. Her body trembled slightly. She was alive.

He didn't see a bullet wound in the back of her head, so where had the blood come from? From Thoreau?

"Rose, honey, talk to me. Are you hurt?"

Slowly she lifted her head just enough for him to see the shock in her eyes.

He brushed her cheek with the pad of his thumb. "He's dead, Rose, it's over."

A small sob escaped her and then she crumpled against him. He scooped her into his arms and carried her back to his car, determined to get her as far away as possible from the man who'd almost taken her life.

TIME BLURRED FOR Rose as Maddox pulled her against him. The numbness that had overcome her when she thought she was about to die had subsided, and now she couldn't stop trembling.

"*Shh*, it's okay, Rose," Maddox murmured. "You're safe. He can't hurt you ever again."

Her head swirled with random thoughts. Thad wasn't the only one who wanted her dead. He'd said it was business.

Someone had paid him to kill her.

But who? And why?

The sound of a siren rent the air, and she closed her eyes, willing away the images of that tree coming toward the car. She'd hoped when they crashed that she'd survive and escape.

But Thad had stirred first and then she'd felt his hands on her and that gun…

"Rose," Maddox said against her ear. "The ambulance is on its way."

She looked at him through a daze, but noticed he had cuts on his face. He'd also limped when he'd carried her to the car. He smelled like smoke and his hand was red, as if it was burned.

"You're hurt," she whispered as reality broke through her own shock.

"The call from Baxter was a setup," he said in a gruff voice. "No one was there."

Rose glanced down at his torn shirt, at the blood on his sleeve. "What happened?"

"I went to search the warehouse, but it exploded."

"*My God*," Rose gasped. "Maddox, someone tried to kill you."

"It was an ambush," he said darkly. "Did Thoreau say anything when he was holding you?"

"Just that it was business to him." She swallowed hard. "Business, as if it didn't bother him to take a life."

"Hit men are trained to be coldhearted," Maddox said. "But you survived, Rose, that's all that matters right now."

She nodded against him, so exhausted from the ordeal that she closed her eyes and leaned against him. The ambulance arrived, doors slamming as the medics got out.

But Thad's cold voice taunted her. He'd confirmed the fact that the Worthingtons weren't her birth parents.

So who were they and what had happened to them?

MADDOX HAD NO remorse over shooting Thoreau.

Except for the fact that Thoreau hadn't talked first. He needed to know who the hell the man had been working for.

On the heels of the ambulance, the ME arrived and Maddox left Rose to be examined while he spoke with Lail.

"Who is the dead man?" Dr. Lail asked.

"He claimed his name was Thad Thoreau, but I think that's an alias. He was a hired gunman."

"I'll run his DNA and prints through the system and look at dental records. I'll let you know when I have something concrete."

"I hope you find something. My search on the prints turned up nothing."

Maddox thanked her, then hurried to check on Rose. The medics were treating her for shock, and she was bruised from the air bag deploying, but she refused to go to the hospital, so they had her sign a waiver.

"You need to look at the sheriff," she told one of the medics. "He's hurt worse than I am."

Maddox shrugged off her concern, but one of the medics looked at his hand and insisted they treat his injuries.

"How is Trina?" Rose asked as they cleaned the cuts on his face.

"My deputy was supposed to go to the store, then follow up with her at the hospital. I haven't heard back yet."

"You need an X-ray for the leg?" the medic asked.

"No, it's just bruised." Maddox assured them they could leave, then he helped Rose into his car.

"Take me to the hospital," Rose said. "I need to see Trina and find out what she had to do with Thad."

"What do you mean?"

Pain etched Rose's face. "Apparently she helped him find me."

Maddox narrowed his eyes. "What?"

"She didn't explain," Rose said. "That's why I need to talk to her. I just hope…that she makes it."

So did he. Maybe she could fill in the blanks.

"Did Thoreau admit who he was working for?"

"No, he just laughed at me," Rose said bitterly. "He said he was glad you hadn't figured out the truth yet. He thought…that he was going to kill me and escape."

"So he was definitely working with someone and trying to cover up the past." Maddox laid his hand over hers as he drove. "We got Thoreau. We'll learn the truth about who's behind this, too."

She nodded although she still looked far too pale for comfort. Seconds later, she closed her eyes and lapsed into silence as he drove toward the hospital. He'd thought she might have fallen asleep, but as soon as he parked at the hospital, she unbuckled her seat belt and slid from the car.

Together they walked inside. Maddox's deputy met them

in the waiting room. "She's in surgery," Deputy White-feather said.

Maddox folded his arms. "What's her condition?"

The deputy shrugged his wide shoulders. "They haven't told me anything. They were wheeling her to the OR when I arrived."

Maddox gestured for Rose to sit down. "Will you get her some coffee and stay with her? I'm going to talk to one of the nurses."

Whitefeather nodded, stepped over to the coffee machine and poured Rose a cup of coffee. He handed it to Rose and claimed the chair beside her, while Maddox stopped at the nurses' station, introduced himself and explained the situation. "Do you have an update on Ms. Fields's condition?"

"I'll check." The nurse made a call, her brows furrowed, then looked at him when she hung up. "The doctor is almost finished. The bullet pierced her abdomen, but missed major organs, so she should pull through. She's in recovery but it'll be a few hours before you can see her."

"Thanks." Maddox went to tell Rose.

Relief echoed in her sigh when he shared the news. "I'm glad she'll make it. But I deserve to know the reason she helped Thad. If…she knew what he planned."

A muscle ticked in Maddox's jaw. "If she did, I'll arrest her for being an accomplice to attempted murder."

His phone buzzed, and he checked the number—the Marshals Service, where he'd left a message the night before. "Excuse me, I have to take this."

He grabbed a cup of coffee for himself, then stepped back outside. "This is Sheriff McCullen."

"Yes, this is US Marshal Norton. You left a message last night asking about a man named Baxter."

"Yes." Maddox explained the situation with Thoreau and Rose. "I received a phone call from Baxter regarding a current investigation in Pistol Whip, but when I went to meet him, he didn't show, and the warehouse where we were supposed to meet exploded. CSI is searching the area in case Baxter was there, but I suspect Thoreau posed as Baxter and set a trap for me, that the bomb was meant to kill me so he could get to Rose."

"You're probably right," Norton said. "We don't have a Baxter on our roster."

Damn. "Listen, Marshal Norton, I think Rose Worthington might have been kidnapped as a little girl, that her birth parents either died or entered WITSEC and disappeared."

"I'll check into that."

"I also suspect that she might have witnessed a crime and that's the reason someone is after her now."

"Go on."

"Thoreau had a flyer with a photo of a little girl about four or five on it. The girl disappeared about twenty years ago. He seemed to think Rose was this little girl. I asked the tech team to search for children who went missing about that age twenty years ago."

"Any word on it?"

"Not yet."

"Let me look at our case files," Norton said. "I can speed the process along. Where is Thoreau?"

"The medical examiner is transporting his body to the morgue. Identifying him might help us determine who he was working for." He explained about finding the Worthingtons dead. "I suspect they were using an alias."

"I'll coordinate with the ME and put a rush on the DNA tests, then get back with you ASAP."

He hung up and Maddox returned to Rose. "That was the real US Marshal. He's going to help us now."

Rose acknowledged his comment with a slight nod, but Maddox's phone buzzed—it was Devon Littleton at the lab. "Sheriff McCullen."

"Sheriff, I finally identified the couple you found at the Worthington house. Their real names were Lloyd and Millie Curtain. At one time, they also went by the last name Kern."

"What else?"

"They were wanted for questioning in regards to a possible money-laundering scheme but disappeared twenty years ago without a word to anyone."

Chapter Seventeen

Rose wanted to speak to Trina, but the doctor insisted that she be sedated, so she'd be incoherent for hours.

"I locked up Vintage Treasures when the ambulance left with Ms. Fields," Deputy Whitefeather said.

"Thank you. I guess I need to go by and clean up." She heaved a weary breath. Trina's blood would be on the floor...

"I'll send a crime cleanup team to take care of it," Maddox said as he approached.

His protective tone touched something deep inside her.

"Come on, I'll drive you home." He glanced at his deputy. "Stay here and guard Trina Fields's room just in case Thoreau's accomplice decides that she might know something valuable and try to silence her."

Rose tensed. She hadn't considered the fact that Trina might still be in danger. If she only knew why the young woman had helped Thad... Had they been romantically involved? Had he paid Trina?

And who did Thad work for?

"Also, call me when she wakes up," Maddox said. "I need to question her about Thoreau."

Whitefeather agreed, and Maddox touched Rose's arm to help her up. She seemed shaky as they walked out to his car. A strained silence fell between them as he drove to her house.

When they arrived, he insisted she stay in the car until he searched the rooms. She twisted her hands together while she waited. A few days ago, she'd thought she had a future with someone who loved her.

Now she was running for her life, had lost the only two people she knew as family and was questioning everything about her life and her past.

Maddox stepped to the porch and motioned that the house was safe, and she dragged herself out and walked up the steps.

Evening shadows streaked his rugged face, the cuts and bruises stark. His tattered clothes, the blood on his shirt, the stench of smoke—all of it was a reminder of the horror in her life.

Yet even bruised and battered with dirt on his hands and clothes, he looked incredibly handsome and strong, as if his arms offered the sanctuary she desperately needed tonight.

MADDOX NEEDED TO talk to Rose about the lab report, but she looked as if she might collapse at any moment.

"Why don't you take a warm bath," he suggested. "I can make us something to eat."

"I'm not hungry," Rose said with a frown as if the thought of food repulsed her.

"All right, clean up." Maddox gestured toward his dirty shirt. "I have another change of clothes in my car. Is it all right if I use your shower downstairs?"

"Of course."

He ached to comfort her, but he stood stock-still as he watched her disappear up the steps.

He retrieved his duffel bag from the trunk of his car, brought it inside and showered, then went to the kitchen. Rose was still upstairs, so he dug in her refrigerator and pulled out ingredients for an omelet. Peppers, onions, spinach, cheese—it took him only a few minutes. While it cooked, he phoned the ranch and spoke to Mama Mary to check on his father.

By the time Rose appeared, wrapped in a big robe with her hair damp and piled on top of her head, he'd set the table.

"You didn't have to do this," Rose said softly.

"I was hungry. And you'll feel better if you have something in your stomach."

Rose gave him a strained smile, then sank into the chair and began to eat. Maddox joined her, and they finished the simple meal in silence.

"I keep thinking about Trina," Rose said. "I don't understand why she helped Thad."

"Don't think about it tonight. Besides, he could have lied about that or lied to her just like he lied to you."

"I suppose you're right," she said although she didn't sound convinced.

"We'll talk to her in the morning." Maddox took her hands in his and helped her from the table, then led her to the den. He pulled her down onto the sofa, then walked over to the bar in the corner and poured her a glass of red wine and himself a scotch.

"I got a call from the lab. They identified your parents— the Worthingtons' real name was Curtain. They were wanted for questioning in a money-laundering scheme twenty years ago."

Rose released a weary breath. "So they were criminals?"

"We don't know that yet. They could have been witnesses."

She looked shell-shocked. He couldn't blame her.

Her hand trembled slightly as she accepted the glass and took a sip. "How's your leg?"

"It's just bruised," he said. "I've had worse from a horse fall."

"Do you need to go home and check on your father?"

"I called and Mama Mary said he's had a good day. I think the anticipation of seeing Brett and Ray has given him a burst of energy."

"That's understandable," Rose said. "But if you need to go home, I understand."

He was taunted by an image of Rose on the ground with that gun so close to her head. He sipped his scotch, then set the highball glass on the coffee table and cradled her hands in his. "What I need is to be here with you. To make sure you're safe."

And alive.

He didn't think he could bear it if she'd died today.

If she had, a little part of him would have died, too.

Emotions he shouldn't feel engulfed him. Emotions that made him want to hold Rose close and never let her go.

Her troubled gaze met his, and a sensual longing sparked in the depths of her eyes. A need that mirrored his own.

Unable to resist the hunger ripping at him, he cupped her face in his hands and closed his mouth over hers.

The kiss was meant to comfort. To remind himself that she was alive. That he hadn't lost her today.

But when she teased his lips with her tongue and threaded her hands in his hair and groaned his name, he lost himself in the moment.

ROSE ABSORBED MADDOX's strength and warmth as he wrapped her in his arms. His kiss felt tentative, gentle, tender, yet when she returned the kiss, passion rose to the surface and hunger flooded her.

She had almost died today. So had Maddox.

Nothing mattered at the moment but that they were alive.

And Maddox made her feel more alive than she ever had in her life.

Thad's kisses had been meant to charm. Maddox's were filled with tenderness, yet also with raw masculine desire.

His hands trailed over her shoulders and down her back, and he pulled her closer. Rose leaned into him, raked her hands along his arms and inhaled the fresh scent of soap and man, driving her to deepen the kiss.

A small groan of pleasure rumbled from his throat, his breath ragged as he eased his lips from hers. "Rose?"

"*Shh*, don't talk, just hold me," she whispered.

"I don't want to take advantage of you."

"You aren't," she said softly. "We both almost died today. You make me feel alive. I need that now."

She took his hand and led him to the bedroom, then removed his gun from his holster and laid it on her nightstand. "I want you, Maddox."

He cupped her face with one hand, his eyes dark and intense as he studied her. She silently pleaded with him to make love to her and pulled his rugged face toward her.

Another groan escaped him, then another one rough with the sound of submission.

A smile warmed her insides as he gave into the hunger between them, and kissed her again. The kiss turned hot, desperate, needy, and made her heart pound with excitement.

She raked her hands down his chest and reached for his shirt, easing open the buttons until she could peel it back and feel his bare chest. *God, his skin felt heavenly, his chest broad and packed with muscle.*

He planted kisses along her throat and neck, nibbled at her ear, whispered a sound of male desire, spiking her own fever.

She tugged off his shirt, revealing broad shoulders, muscular arms and a torso dusted with dark hair. Rose dropped kisses along his chest, her fingers dancing across it in a sensuous parade that made him suck in his breath.

He slowly untied her robe belt and slid it over her shoulders, then kissed her neck again as one hand cupped her breasts. Her nipples budded beneath his touch, aching for more.

Seconds later, their touches turned frantic, passionate, and he tore off her gown and shucked his jeans.

The sight of his nearly naked body stole her breath. The bruises on his body reminded her that he'd almost given his life to save her today.

All the more reason she wanted to be with him now.

Hunger for him triggered a desperation that she'd never felt before. And when he closed his lips over one pebbled nipple, she closed her eyes, sensations spiraling through her as her body teemed with pleasure.

MADDOX ORDERED HIMSELF to stop this madness, but even as he did so, he trailed his tongue across Rose's breasts and peeled her panties down her legs. He wanted her so badly his sex throbbed to be inside her, his heart racing with the urgency to have her.

She clung to him, her hunger palpable in the soft moans she elicited, her hands urging him closer as he rose above her. Needing to taste her, he planted kisses down her breasts to her stomach, then slid his fingers down to her heat.

She arched against him and stroked his calf with her foot, then wrapped one leg around him, urging him between her thighs.

His body hardened, and he rocked himself against her, teasing her femininity with his erection. Her breathing grew ragged, hurried with excitement, and he moved down her body and parted her thighs with his hands.

Then he closed his lips over her heat.

Rose dug her fingers into his hair and murmured a soft

"yes," her body quivering as he teased and tormented her with his tongue. And when he lifted her hips to taste her sweetness, she cried out his name and came with a fierceness that almost sent him over the edge.

He let her ride the wave of pleasure, his own spiked by the sound of her whispering his name, and he grabbed a condom from his jeans on the floor and rolled it on, then rose above her, kneed her legs apart and nudged her with his hard length.

Rose slipped her hand down to stroke him, and mindless sensations ripped through him.

He stroked her over and over, his blood on fire as she guided him inside her. The moment he felt her body clench around his, his own release was imminent. But he prolonged the pleasure as long as he could, easing out of her and thrusting inside her warmth again and again. Finally he lifted her hips to angle her so he could drive himself deeper, until he filled her and she cried out again with another orgasm.

He came then, swiftly, intensely, and he gripped her hips and closed his eyes, emotions pummeling him as she completed him.

ROSE'S BODY QUIVERED with sensations as she curled into Maddox's arms.

Making love with him had been intense, mind-numbing and so erotic that she never wanted it to end. He wrapped his arm around her and stroked her hair, his strong arms a fortress that would protect her from the world.

"Rose?"

"*Shh*, don't say anything," she whispered. "I just want to lie here and block out the world."

He murmured his understanding, tucked her up against him so her chest touched his, then kissed the top of her head. Rose savored being safe for the moment and banished other thoughts from her head.

Tomorrow she and Maddox would face the questions again.

Tonight she just wanted to sleep in his arms and savor the pleasure he'd given her.

DAMMIT TO HELL. Thoreau was dead.

But Rose and that sheriff were still alive.

He watched her house from his car, his gut churning. The big announcement would come any day now. They had so much riding on it that he couldn't take the chance on Rose's memory returning.

He had to do something. Although he felt antsy over the idea of getting his own hands dirty.

But he'd come too far to turn back now. If Rose remembered what she'd seen twenty years ago, if she remembered him or his father, his life would be ruined.

So would his family's.

And that was not an option.

Setting fire to Rose's house would work. Kill her and McCullen together.

Sweat trickled down the back of his neck. He glanced up and down the road, making sure no other cars were around. The lights were off in the house, the bedroom dark.

Tugging the hoodie up over his head, he slipped from the car. He retrieved the gas can and his matches from the trunk, then crept through the bushes to the side of the house. He doused the outside wall and grass with the gas, then spread it all along the back wall to the opposite side. Too dangerous to do the front. Someone might drive up.

His pulse hammered as he struck a match and dropped it onto the gas. The fire ignited within seconds. He hurried to the far wall, then dropped another match, smiling as it sparked, and the fire began to ripple along the house, crackling and popping as it ate the wood.

One last match and he darted back through the bushes and slipped inside his vehicle to watch the house erupt into flames.

Chapter Eighteen

The strong smell of smoke jarred Maddox from sleep.

He sat up and looked around the bedroom, confused momentarily by the dark. He was in Rose's bed. They'd made love and had fallen asleep.

Was he dreaming about a fire?

He slid from bed and eased toward the closed door, and felt it. Not hot but…the smell of smoke was stronger.

The hair on the back of his neck stood on end as he pulled it open. Just as he feared, smoke seeped up the stairs.

Instantly on alert, he ran to Rose and shook her. "Rose, the house is on fire. We need to get out."

"What?" Rose vaulted up, eyes wide with panic.

"There's smoke downstairs." Maddox yanked on his jeans and shirt, then grabbed his gun from the nightstand. Rose took his cue, grabbed her clothes and hurriedly dressed.

Maddox snatched his phone and called 911. "The house is on fire. Get the fire department here now!"

Rose hurried to the door and followed him into the hall. They started down the steps, smoke clogging the air and nearly blinding them. When they reached the landing, he glanced at the hall. The back area was filled with smoke, but the front of the house was slightly clearer.

Flames crawled into the den along the floor, shooting upward and eating the drapes.

Rose started toward the mantel. "My music boxes," Rose said, choking on a cry.

Maddox yanked on her hand. "We have to get out first."

But Rose jerked away to retrieve the music boxes. "No, they're all I have left of my mother!"

"I'll come back and get them." Heat speared his arms and hands as he glanced into the kitchen. Flames rippled along the floor and walls, swirling higher. The smoke grew thicker, stinging his eyes.

The sheer curtains were ablaze. Wood crackled and popped, and a board snapped from the ceiling and crashed down. Rose coughed and stumbled, but he caught her, curving his arm around her to steady her as he coaxed her toward the door. "Come on. It's spreading fast."

Remembering the trap he'd walked into at the warehouse, he cautiously opened the front door, drew his weapon and scanned the yard. What if the killer had started the fire to draw them out so he could kill them?

ROSE COVERED HER MOUTH, desperately trying not to inhale smoke. Behind her, the fire was eating her house alive.

After all that had happened, she shouldn't let it upset her. The only things of sentimental value in the house were the music boxes. The thought of losing them made tears sting her eyes.

She wanted to turn back and get them, but flames were licking at the sofa and chair, feeding on the fabric. The room was so thick with smoke, she could hardly see the mantel now.

Maddox tugged at her hand. "Come on, but stay low, Rose. Whoever set this could be waiting outside to ambush us."

Fear clawed at Rose. He was right. The killer had been

cunning enough to lure Maddox to that warehouse. He could be here now watching, just waiting on them to run out.

Terrified, she stooped low, staying behind Maddox as they darted through the room, then out the door and across the driveway. He opened the door to his car and ushered her inside. "Stay down."

She ducked in the seat, burying her head in her hands as he scanned the area. Seconds later, a siren wailed, tires screeching as a fire engine roared closer and swung into her driveway.

Maddox hurried to meet the firefighters, and she watched from the safety of the car as they vaulted into action and dragged hoses toward the house.

Maddox ran back to her and leaned into the car. "Are you okay?"

Rose nodded although she wasn't okay at all. How could she be?

Flames burst from the roof of the house, glowing bright in the early morning light, windows shattering and wood crackling as the fire raged out of control.

"I'll be right back."

Rose clenched her hands together and watched in horror as Maddox darted up the drive and ran back into the house. One of the firefighters tried to stop him, but he forged ahead, the fireman on his trail.

The firefighters were shouting orders, dumping water on the flames, but it was a lost cause. The roof in the back of the house caved in with a thunderous roar.

Rose scanned the front lawn. *Was Maddox all right? Had he survived the bomb at the warehouse only to die now?*

Anxious, she paced across the grass. It seemed like hours, but was probably only minutes later when he finally emerged.

Her heart swelled with emotions. His face was streaked with dirt and soot, his clothes dotted with ashes but his arms were full.

He'd kept his word and saved her music boxes.

MADDOX CARRIED AS MANY of the music boxes as he could while the firefighter had grabbed the remaining ones. It had been stupid as hell to go back inside.

But the antiques meant so much to Rose that he couldn't bear for her to lose them. Not after she'd already lost so much.

She ran toward him, her face pale. Still, the gratitude in her eyes made it worth the risk he'd taken as he set the music boxes on the ground.

She threw her arms around him. "Maddox…you could have died in there."

"I'm fine," he said, his voice hoarse with smoke.

"How did the fire get started?" one of the firefighters asked.

Maddox gritted his teeth. "My guess, it was arson. I want the fire investigator to search for an accelerant." His explanation about the earlier attacks on Rose was met with a scowl.

"I'll call the fire chief and get him out here right away."

"Thanks." He stepped to the side to make the call, and Maddox buzzed Hoberman. "Yes, I want the scene gone over inch by inch. Maybe he messed up this time and we'll find some evidence to nail him."

"I'll be right there with a crew."

Maddox hung up and turned to see Rose sitting on the lawn with the music boxes around her, watching her house disintegrate.

The next two hours were chaos. The fire chief arrived and began combing the place, then Hoberman and his team rolled up.

Hoberman cornered Maddox. "I talked to Littleton. He finally got something on Thoreau."

"What did he find out?"

"Thoreau's real name was Jim Hinley. He was former military, a sniper. Five years ago, he got out of the army and decided to make his living using the skills he'd learned in the service."

"Did he have any family? Parents? A wife?"

"No," Hoberman said. "Mother died before he joined the service. And he was never married. I talked to his commanding officer and he said the guy didn't make friends. Was a real loner."

So he fit the profile of a killer—no personal connections.

Hoberman went to meet his crime team and start processing the remains of the house. Maddox headed over to the fire chief. "Find anything yet?"

"Yeah, a gas can." The fire chief lifted his hat and raked a hand through his hair. "Looks like the perpetrator poured gas all along the outside of the house, then lit a match."

Son of a bitch.

Bitterness at the man who'd tormented Rose, and taken her home from her, enraged Maddox.

If—no, *when*—he found this guy he might just kill him instead of putting him in handcuffs.

THE MORNING PASSED like a horror show as Rose watched the crime scene workers and firefighters try to salvage her home and process the ruins.

Maddox stood by, overseeing the situation and offering her comforting looks, but the reality was that her house was gone, her belongings were gone and the only parents she'd ever known were gone.

She was alone.

Even the one friend she'd made in town had betrayed her.

Maddox insisted on driving her to his ranch, although first they stopped at the general store so she could pick up toiletries and a few necessities.

She chose the items on autopilot, simple T-shirts and a couple of pairs of jeans. At this point, clothes were unimportant. Surviving and figuring out the truth about her past was all that mattered.

When they arrived at Maddox's ranch, the beauty of the land compared to the smoky rubble of her rental house brought a wave of sadness and longing for a home of her own. One she actually owned, not one she just rented because her parents had trained her not to get attached to anything. A real home with sweet memories and family and people who loved her.

Mama Mary welcomed her with a hug. Maddox explained about the fire, and Mama Mary ushered Rose to the guest room on the second floor, coaxed her into the bathroom for a warm bath and promised her breakfast when she was ready.

Rose ran some hot water, poured in the bubble bath Mama Mary had left for her, and sank into the tub. She closed her eyes, letting the bath soothe her and wash away the stench of the fire.

But she couldn't wash away the fear consuming her or the reality that someone still wanted her dead.

Finally, when the water cooled, she dressed and walked down the steps. Mama Mary was pouring coffee into a mug and handed it to her. "Sit down here, honey, and relax. Maddox is visiting with his daddy. He'll be down in a minute."

Rose sipped the coffee, once again warmed by the comfortable furniture, the homey scents of sausage and bacon cooking, and the photos of the McCullen boys.

She didn't know what kind of men his brothers had grown up to be, but Maddox was a strong, admirable man.

He'd run into a burning house to save her music boxes.

No man had ever done anything so heroic for her.

The memory of the way he'd held her and made love to her played through her head, rousing other emotions, and her heart fluttered with longing for another evening in his arms.

Footsteps sounded, and Maddox entered the room, dressed in a fresh chambray shirt and jeans, his damp hair combed back, his rugged face cleanly shaven. *God, he was handsome.*

She couldn't take her eyes off him as he gave Mama Mary a hug, accepted a mug of coffee and joined her at the table for breakfast.

In spite of the fear still pressing against her chest, she offered Maddox a tentative smile. His dark gaze settled on her, the corner of his mouth twitching as if he wanted to smile but knew that she'd been through hell and he needed to give her time to recover.

Dear Lord...she was falling in love with him.

The thought jolted her, sending fear streaking through her. She couldn't fall in love with Maddox or any other man.

Loving someone meant losing them, and she couldn't bear any more pain than she'd already had.

MADDOX WASHED HIS food down with coffee, grateful Mama Mary had taken care of Rose while he visited with his father. Meanwhile, Marshal Norton had phoned saying they needed to talk.

Rose thanked Mama Mary, and so did he. Then he stood. "That marshal is on his way here. If you want, you can wait with Mama Mary in the kitchen. Or if you need to lie down, you're welcome to the guest room."

"No, Maddox," Rose said firmly. "I can't run from the questions or the truth, we both know that." Her chin lifted defiantly. "You may think I'm weak, but I can face whatever happens."

"No one said you were weak," Maddox said gruffly. "Frankly, under the circumstances you've held up extremely well."

The doorbell chimed, and she followed him to the door. Marshal Norton was a tall, thin man with a goatee. He was dressed in jeans, a western tie and shirt and a Stetson. They made quick introductions, and the marshal flashed his identification. Maddox scrutinized it carefully. He'd been fooled by that phone call. No way would he be fooled again.

Satisfied the ID looked real, Maddox led them both to the office he shared with his father, the one that would soon be his when his father passed.

Unless his brothers came back to stay...

He bit the inside of his cheek. He didn't have time to think about that now.

Marshal Norton's eyes flashed with interest as he looked at Rose, and Maddox gritted his teeth. *Damn, he'd never been a jealous man.*

Because he'd never cared about a woman before.

And he cared about Rose?

God yes, he cared about her.

"Miss Worthington, I'm glad to meet you," the marshal said.

Rose gave him a wary look. "I wish I could say the same. But I never thought I'd be dealing with the law, especially the US Marshals Service."

"I'm sorry," Norton said. "But we do need to talk."

Maddox offered the man coffee, but he declined. He and

Rose seated themselves on the sofa while Norton claimed the leather wing chair by the oak coffee table.

Now the man was here, Maddox was anxious to get the ball rolling. The sooner they knew the truth, the sooner he could solve this case and Rose would be safe. "You said you have information."

A vein in Norton's neck bulged. "Yes. The prints at the Worthingtons' house registered." He faced Rose, his hands folded, his expression grim. "The people who raised you, the Worthingtons, were not your birth parents. Their real names were Millie and Lloyd Curtain."

"The ME already gave us their names," Maddox said.

Rose rubbed at her temple. "What happened to my birth parents? And how did I come to live with the Worthingtons?"

"They kidnapped you from a foster home when you were four."

Maddox reached over to put a hand on Rose's shoulder, but she stiffened and shrugged it off. "Why would they take me?" Rose asked in a raw whisper.

"Because your birth parents were murdered."

Chapter Nineteen

Rose clenched her hands. Her birth parents had been murdered? "Who killed them? And why?"

"We don't know details yet, but we have suspicions."

"Then tell us what you do know, and what your theory is," Maddox interjected. "And start from the beginning. Rose was the girl in that photo on the milk carton?"

Norton nodded, then angled his head toward Rose "Yes. Your birth parents' names are Donna and Keith Hudgens."

"And my name?" Rose asked.

"Hailey."

Hailey Hudgens. Rose gulped, then rolled the name over and over in her head. "Why don't I remember them?"

A pregnant pause, then Norton cleared his throat. "We believe you witnessed their murder. The doctors at the hospital said you were traumatized by their deaths."

Rose struggled with his declaration. That dream she'd had that had seemed so real—it must have been her memory returning. But she didn't feel like sharing that yet. She wanted more information from the marshal.

Maddox cleared his throat. "So what happened to the Hudgenses? Where are they buried?"

"Actually we didn't know where they were, not until you found those remains on the cabin property."

Rose gasped. "The skeleton in the storm shelter and the one in the grave were my parents?"

"Yes."

"If you don't know who killed them," Maddox asked, "do you know the reason they were murdered?"

Norton folded his hands on his knees. "We believe the Hudgenses and Curtains—Worthingtons—were partners, that they were working with a theft ring that stole over a million dollars. We think your birth parents tried to swindle one of their partners and he killed them."

Nausea bubbled in Rose's throat. "My parents were criminals?"

"That's our theory," Norton said. "A neighbor called to report a disturbance at the house. When the local sheriff arrived, he found you, Rose—well the little girl Hailey— alone in the house. She was hiding in the closet, but she had blood on her hands and there was blood all over the house."

Rose stared down at her hands. The images of the red spraying on the wall and floors flashed through her mind.

Norton turned to Rose. "*You* were traumatized, so they took you to the hospital and treated you for shock. Your parents' bodies were not in the house, but due to the amount of blood, police believed they were dead. Social services placed you in a foster home. Two days after that, the Curtains kidnapped you and disappeared under the name of Kern. During their escape, they had an accident, which landed you in the hospital and drew suspicion from the police so the couple took you and ran again. That's when they became the Worthingtons."

"I still can't believe this," Rose whispered.

"The sheriff had reported the kidnapping and had your face put on the milk carton hoping someone would recognize you, but nothing ever came of it."

"Because my parents, the Worthingtons, kept such a low profile," Rose said.

Maddox nodded. "Until Thad Thoreau found you," Maddox said. "Or whoever he was working with did."

Norton nodded.

Maddox folded his hands. "Were the Worthingtons in WITSEC?"

The marshal shook his head.

"Do you know who killed them?" Maddox asked.

"No." He addressed Rose. "Actually we thought you might be able to help us with that."

"I wish I could but I don't remember anything." A dozen questions niggled at Rose's mind. "And why come after me now? It's been twenty years, and I didn't remember anything."

"Whoever killed your birth parents probably thinks you can identify him, or that you know what they did with the stolen money. It's also possible the killer believes the Worthingtons took the money, and that you might have it."

"But I don't," Rose said instantly. "My parents, I mean the Worthingtons, lived a very frugal life. They didn't even have a savings account."

"The Worthingtons could have hidden the money," Maddox suggested. "Spending it would have drawn attention to them, something they wanted to avoid since they were using assumed identities and were on the run."

That made sense. And it explained the reason they hadn't wanted her to participate in activities that would garner attention. The reason they hadn't encouraged close friendships.

Which meant her entire life had been a lie.

MADDOX UNDERSTOOD THAT Rose needed time to process the revelations Marshal Norton had just dumped on her. "Did you search the cabin property for the money?"

"We did," Norton said. "We also searched the house where the Worthingtons were killed and the house where the Hudgenses lived, but found nothing. We didn't find any hidden bank accounts, either."

Rose walked over to the window and looked outside for a moment, her body rigid.

The marshal lowered his voice. "Has she talked to you about what happened when she was little?"

Maddox shook his head. Although she had had that nightmare… "No. She said she doesn't remember anything before she lived with the Worthingtons."

What would it do to her psyche to push her to remember now?

Rose turned back to face them, her arms crossed. "Do you have a photograph of my birth parents?"

"I can find one," Marshal Norton said.

"Then get it. I want to see it."

Norton pulled his tablet from the inside of his jacket, set it on his lap and accessed his files. Seconds later, he angled the screen to face Rose.

"Here is a photograph of the Hudgenses."

Maddox watched pain flicker across Rose's face. She resembled her birth mother, with her wavy hair and petite build, while her father was tall with an angular face, sandy brown hair and a mustache.

"Mrs. Hudgens was thirty-one, Mr. Hudgens thirty-four at the time of their murder," Marshal Norton said.

Rose seemed to soak in their features, a sad look washing over her. "They look so normal, not like criminals." She glanced up at the marshal. "What did they do for a living?"

"Your mother was a stay-at-home mom," he said. "Mr. Hudgens was an accountant."

"So he had access to other people's money?" Rose said.

"Yes."

"But you have no proof that the Hudgenses actually stole anything?" Rose asked.

Maddox grimaced. Rose was obviously in denial and didn't want to face the fact that the people who'd given birth to her and the couple who'd raised her were involved in illegal activities. Who could blame her?

"I'm not at liberty to discuss specifics," Norton said, "but we have a theory."

Maddox silently cursed. *Why the hell couldn't all the law enforcement agencies work together?* The feds and marshals always treated local sheriffs as if they were morons. He didn't like it worth a damn.

Rose's breath hitched, the sound shaky in the silence. "You have the address of the house where my birth parents were murdered?"

Norton arched a brow. "Yes."

"Give it to me." She turned to Maddox. "Maybe if I see that house I'll remember something about their murder and the man who killed them."

ROSE REMEMBERED HOW safe she'd felt in Maddox's arms the night before, how tender yet passionate his lovemaking was, and she wanted to crawl back in his arms again.

To lie with him and have him hold her and make love to her and help her forget the horror of what she'd just learned.

That her birth parents and the people who'd raised her might have been fugitives. That instead of protecting her, the Worthingtons had kidnapped her and gone on the run to avoid prison.

"Thank you for coming," Maddox told the marshal.

Marshal Norton stood and shook Maddox's hand, then clasped Rose's between both of his. "I know this is all a shock to you, but if you remember anything about your childhood or your parents or anyone who might have visited them, please call me."

"I will." Rose turned to Maddox. "Maddox, will you take me to the house?" She couldn't bear to call the Hudgenses her parents.

She didn't remember them. Didn't know them.

Maybe she never would remember them.

Part of her wanted to bury her head in the sand, but she couldn't do that. She needed to face the truth in order to move on.

Besides, if she recognized the person who'd killed the Hudgenses, she could send their killer to prison.

Maddox walked the marshal to the door, then returned to the study. He looked worried. "Are you sure you're up to this, Rose?"

"Yes. I need to do this, Maddox," Rose said. "If you don't want to drive me, I'll go by myself."

"No way in hell," Maddox muttered, his voice gruff. "It's too dangerous."

Maddox retrieved his keys from the desk and rushed to tell Mama Mary where they were going. Then they walked outside to his car. The sunlight was waning, storm clouds playing across the land.

Several horses ran free in the pasture, their manes blowing in the wind. They lapsed into a strained quiet as Maddox drove down the long drive to the highway and headed toward Rose's childhood home.

The house where she'd lived with the Hudgenses until they were murdered and she'd been left alone.

Tumultuous emotions churned inside her. She should feel relieved to know why she and the Worthingtons—Curtains—had never been close. Why she'd never quite felt like she belonged with them.

Instead she felt empty inside and more alone than ever.

MADDOX CONTEMPLATED THE facts of the case. Rose needed time to assimilate the information she'd received and process the idea that both couples who'd called themselves her parents had been in trouble with the law.

She stared out the window as night fell and the wind

picked up. Dead leaves swirled across the parched ground, dust blowing across the highway.

He passed an older wood-framed house set back from the road, then drove a mile to the end, where another wood-framed house sat among overgrown scrub brush and weeds. The roof needed repairs, the shutters were rotting and several windowpanes were broken.

"Do you recognize any of this?" Maddox asked.

Rose massaged that scar, her jaw tightening. "No...I don't think so."

Maddox parked in the graveled drive, worry knotting his belly. "Don't push too hard, Rose. You may not have seen the killer's face that night."

Rose twisted her hands together. "But what if I did? Maybe I've known all along who took my family from me, and I could have sent their killer to prison."

"You were just a child, Rose. An innocent little girl. You had to be terrified."

Her eyes looked tormented. "That nightmare I had the other night...I was remembering. I was hiding in a closet. I heard my father shouting, my mother screaming...I saw the blood."

Maddox went still, but kept his voice calm. "What else do you remember?"

Rose rubbed her forehead. "I don't know...the rest is a fog." A haunted look streaked her eyes as she turned to stare at the house. "What if it was the Worthingtons—I mean the Curtains, Maddox? What if the people who pretended to be my family all these years actually murdered my birth parents?"

Chapter Twenty

Rose struggled to recall some detail of the house where she'd supposedly spent the first four years of her life.

But nothing seemed familiar.

The skeletal frame looked old and dilapidated, the wood was mud-splattered and aged, the front yard a minefield of weeds and scrub brush. Three windowpanes were broken, either from storms or from vandals.

Maybe teens had broken in to use the vacant house for a party—or the person who'd killed her parents had done it when they were searching for the money her mother and father had stolen.

Embezzlement? Money-laundering?

Although that marshal hadn't revealed any specifics about who they'd robbed.

Maybe it wasn't true. Her parents—both sets—could have been innocent. Or was that wishful thinking on her part?

"Rose?"

She slid from the car. "I'm going in."

"Are you sure about this?" Maddox asked as he followed her up to the front door.

"I'm sure I have to know the truth," she said, resigned to whatever she might discover. "Whether I'm Hailey Hudgens or Rose Worthington—"

He gently gripped her arms. "It doesn't matter what your name is, Rose, nothing can change who you are on the inside."

Rose angled her head to look at him, emboldened by his words. "Thank you for saying that, Maddox. But we both know I can't walk away. Facing the past may be the only thing that will keep me alive."

A second passed where he could have challenged her, but he knew she was right, and that realization was reflected in his eyes.

She turned the doorknob, a cold draft blasting her as she stepped inside. The door screeched as if it hadn't been oiled in ages, the brown linoleum was worn and bowed from water damage, and a musty odor permeated the air.

Dust motes floated in the sliver of light seeping through the broken window, the particles dancing like ghosts as the wind swirled them around the vacant room.

Rose paused to study the worn plaid couch, the ugly green chair with the stuffing hanging out as if an animal had chewed on it, and the mice droppings in the corner. The walls were a dingy, yellowed white and marred with dirt, and the ceiling was dark with water stains.

She tried to picture herself on that couch with her parents, but the image wouldn't surface.

Maddox's footsteps behind her startled her, and she jumped.

"I'm sorry, Rose. The place looks deserted, but I want to do a quick walk-through to make sure no one's inside."

She let him move past her, grateful for his presence and praying that some familiar memory would surface from the empty void in her mind.

She studied the room more intently as he searched the house. Had she watched shows on that television as a child?

"It's clear," Maddox said. "Although I'll warn you, Rose,

the place hasn't been cleaned since the Hudgenses were shot here. If you don't want—"

"Stop trying to change my mind," she said firmly. Nerves rippled along her spine though, as she considered his statement.

"I'll give you a few minutes," Maddox said in a low voice.

She murmured her thanks, then crossed the threshold of the door to look into the kitchen. An orange Formica table with four metal chairs occupied one corner, the only furniture in the dingy room. The green walls had faded to a putrid color, the outdated cabinets were coated with grease and dust. The gold stove and refrigerator had to be the originals, and when she opened one of the cabinets, she found canned goods that were outdated by at least a decade.

She closed her eyes, wracking her brain. Had she and her mother and father eaten homey meals around this table? Had her mother liked to cook? Had she celebrated her birthdays in this house? Woken up to see toys Santa had left? Made sugar cookies with her mother and ridden horsey on her daddy's back?

If so, why couldn't she remember any of it? She didn't even know if her parents had loved her...

And if they'd stolen money, as Marshal Norton suggested, what had they done with it?

MADDOX GRIMACED AT the blood stained floor and walls.

But the detective in him was excited by the possibility. He phoned the marshal.

Marshal Norton answered on the second ring. "Did Rose remember anything?"

"Not yet," Maddox said. "Do you have the original reports from the sheriff who investigated the Hudgenses' case?"

"Yes."

"What kind of forensic evidence was found?"

"Hang on and let me access the records." A couple of minutes passed, then he returned to the line. "A partial print from the front door. Blood samples were collected that matched the couple's."

"I'm going to call a team out here and have them process this place again. The original team could have missed something. With the advances in technology, we might be able to identify the fibers and blood and whatever else we find more clearly than they could twenty years ago."

"Okay, send me the results."

Maddox hung up, phoned Hoberman and explained what he needed.

"I'll get my best guys out there now," Hoberman said.

ROSE LOOKED DOWN at the scarred sink, and for a moment saw the water running. Then a woman's hands washing tomatoes. Music played softly in the background from a radio in the corner, sweeping her back twenty years.

But the music was in her head, an old big band tune. For a moment, images surfaced—a man and woman dancing in the kitchen...her parents. Her father leading her mother around the room, her mother's skirt swirling around her ankles as they swayed back and forth together.

Tears burned the backs of her eyelids. She couldn't see their faces well, but she felt the love between them, the peace inside the old house as if it didn't matter if they had money or nice things.

As if they couldn't possibly be guilty of the crime Norton had mentioned.

But the image faded as quickly as it had come.

A tremor rippled through her, and she ran her finger along the counter, but a noise outside made her jerk her head up. She glanced through the kitchen window, and saw a tire swing attached to a large tree by a rope.

Her vision blurred again, another image surfacing from the past. The tire was swinging back and forth, creaking in the wind. A little boy about eight years old with brown hair and freckles gripped the rope, laughing as he tried to make it go faster.

Wind rustled the leaves on the ground and shook the tree branches. She felt that wind in her hair, on her cheek, and a chill rippled through her. She was outside playing with that little boy. He yelled her name, and she ran over to him and gave him a big push.

A man's loud voice yelled at the boy from inside the house, and Rose realized the man was his father. He was inside with her parents.

A shudder tore through her as the memory floated away, and she rubbed her arms to ward off the chill. Who was the little boy? And the man? Were they neighbors? Friends of her family's?

She made her way through the kitchen and veered into the hallway. Instinctively she knew the house had three bedrooms. The one on the right belonged to her parents, the one across had been hers. The back room had been empty.

In her dream, she'd hidden in the closet—but which one? The closet in her room?

Her lungs strained for air as she glanced into her childhood bedroom. It seemed familiar…yet fuzzy at the same time. A worn pink spread covered a twin bed. Stuffed animals that had been pecked at by birds were scattered about, the stuffing leaking out. The pink checkered curtains hung askew, faded and stained from time, and rain had seeped through the broken pane.

A small battered pine dresser stood in the corner, a pink jewelry box on top. Before she even opened it, she knew a tiny ballerina was inside, that she would twirl and dance to "Over the Rainbow."

A wave of sadness mushroomed inside her when she

lifted the lid and saw the ballerina dancing. Once again time sucked her backward, and she saw a little girl lying on the bed hugging her teddy bear while she whispered secrets in its ear. Then another image of her playing in the costume jewelry her mother had given her, and the paper dolls on the floor.

The trunk at the foot of the bed held dress-up clothes, things her mother had bought for next to nothing at thrift stores and garage sales.

Rose kneeled at the trunk and opened it, dust swirling upward and floating away to reveal the vintage garments. One day in particular struck a memory—her mother tugging her hand as they ventured into a small antiques shop. Her mother had squealed when she found the trunk, already holding several ball gowns and prom dresses as well as a fake fur hat and beaded purse.

She had bought the entire trunk and carried it home. Then she'd donned one of the dresses and allowed Rose to put on the other. They'd had a tea party that afternoon with sugar cookies, tea and milk, and pretended they were traveling the world.

The memory brought tears to her eyes. That moment in time had been so special and sweet. How could she have forgotten it?

She touched each of the dresses, holding them to her cheek to feel the soft satin and taffeta. Her birth mother had loved her.

She couldn't have possibly been a criminal. Could she?

Determined to uncover the answer, she placed the clothing back inside and closed the trunk, opened the closet door and surveyed the contents.

A few toddler-sized dresses, a yellow raincoat, rubber boots, a chalkboard, bags of broken crayons and paper so old that it was yellowed. Another box on the floor held socks and pajamas, a bright purple gown, sneakers and a pacifier that must have belonged to her as a baby.

She found another box filled with onesies and infant sleepers and frowned. *Had her mother kept her baby clothes?*

The wind rattled the roof, jarring her from the moment. This closet wasn't the place where she'd hidden.

Sucking in a breath for courage, she stepped into the hallway. She peeked into the third bedroom and was stunned to see a crib, complete with a pink baby blanket and doll inside. Pink ruffled curtains, worn and faded with time, draped the window, and a white dresser held a stack of cloth diapers and infant clothes.

Had those been hers at one time? Although why would her mother have diapers in the house?

Nerves knotted her shoulders as she stepped back into the hall and opened the closet door. A dark raincoat and two winter coats hung there, an umbrella hanging beside them.

Other than that, the closet was empty.

The dreams taunted her. She'd definitely hidden behind clothing, behind what she'd thought were coats.

Perspiration beaded on her neck as she ducked inside her parents' bedroom. A double bed was draped in a faded blue spread, the carpet threadbare and stained.

It took her a moment to realize that those were blood-stains.

Her parents' blood.

This was the room where they'd been shot and…killed.

The dark spots splattered across the floor and into the hall now registered, and she realized that her parents had been bleeding as the shooter had dragged their bodies outside.

Why had he taken their bodies? Why hadn't he left them in the house?

Because he'd wanted to cover his tracks?

The wind beat at the house, rattling the windows and seeping through the cracks of the wooden house, launching Rose back in time…

It was dark outside, dark in the house, dark everywhere. She huddled under her pink blanket, clenching her teddy bear, too afraid to look in the room.

Monsters were everywhere. She dreamed about them all the time—outside the window, tapping at the glass, wanting to come in. Under the bed and in the closet, and sometimes they hid in the bathroom to sneak up on her at night.

Mommy said the monsters weren't real. Daddy told her to be a big girl and to go back to bed. But if she was really quiet, and he was asleep and she tiptoed in their room, Mommy would let her crawl in bed beside her. Mommy would wrap her arms around her and hold her and soothe her with sweet kisses on her cheek and brush her hair back from her face. Mommy smelled good, like flowers and cake batter and sugar cookies.

But Daddy wasn't asleep yet, and he and Mommy had been fighting.

She squeezed her eyes shut, covered her ears and hugged Bitty the Bear so tight she was afraid his insides would squish out. The clock in the hall dinged, and she rocked herself back and forth, waiting it out until the house grew quiet.

Except the wind kept howling, and she was sure it was a monster waiting on her parents to go to sleep so he could steal her from her bed.

Clenching Bitty, she peeked from the covers. She didn't see anything, but that didn't mean it wasn't there. She slid from bed, and ran across the hall. Daddy was still and Mommy was curled on her side facing the wall.

She ducked down low and snuck into the room, then crawled in bed beside her mommy. Mommy curled her arms around her and stroked her hair and she knew she was safe.

But a noise woke her. A loud crash.

Then Mommy shook her. "Hide, Hailey, hurry, run and hide in the closet."

She jumped up, her heart racing. She started to scream, but Mommy covered her mouth with her hand, picked her up and swung her from the bed. "Hurry, hide!"

"Don't make a sound," Daddy hissed.

Her mommy shoved her in the closet and closed the door. She started shaking all over, a sob lodging in her throat.

She pressed her fist over her mouth to keep from crying. Outside the door, footsteps pounded. Shouting started. Her daddy.

Then her mother screamed, "Stop!"

Something shattered on the floor. Other noises. Shouts, furniture being turned over.

Then a gun blast.

She buried her head in her hands and screamed into her arms, terrified. What was happening?

Don't make a sound, her mommy had said. But where was Mommy now? Were she and Daddy okay?

Her legs wobbled, but she stooped on her knees and tried to look through the crack in the door, then her mommy screamed again, and the man grabbed her hair, and she saw red...

Daddy on the bedroom floor, blood everywhere.

Mommy fighting with someone, a big man...a shot going off, Mommy falling...more red... Red coming from Mommy...

Rose jerked her eyes open, trembling, a scream ripping from her throat. God help her...had she seen the man's face?

She closed her eyes again, willing herself to bring him into focus, but another noise rent the air.

Another gunshot. But this one wasn't in her dream. It was real. And it had come from outside the house... Maddox was out there.

Chapter Twenty-One

Maddox darted behind a tree, using the trunk as a shield. Dammit. Who the hell was shooting at him?

The bullet had just grazed his arm, but the shooter fired again, and brush crackled as the man closed in on him.

He peered around the edge of the tree, searching the thicket as he gripped his own gun at the ready. Rose was inside the house...once the bastard got him out of the way, he'd go after her next.

Not going to happen.

He just prayed Rose stayed inside until he could take care of the perp.

A sliver of light seeped through the dense foliage, and he spotted the silhouette of a man creeping toward him.

Maddox aimed his gun at the shadow and fired. The man jumped back and fired another round at him. Suddenly the front door opened, and Rose screamed.

"Maddox!"

"Get back inside, Rose!" He fired in the direction of the shooter again, determined to protect Rose.

She ducked back inside and slammed the screen door, and he raced to the next tree, quickly darting behind it for cover. Another bullet pinged off the bark and whizzed by his face.

Maddox cursed. "Who the hell are you? Why do you want to kill Rose?"

Only the sound of dry leaves rustling broke the tense silence. Maddox glanced at the house and gauged the distance to the door. He wanted inside to protect Rose.

But he'd get shot for sure if he dashed out in the open.

Maybe he could make it around to the back door. Or even a side window.

He peered around the edge of the tree, but another bullet zoomed an inch from his head and he jumped back. He fired again, but his bullet pinged off a pine.

Instead of heading toward the house, he dashed through the brush, hoping to circle far enough behind the perp to sneak up on him. He made it past three more trees, then climbed over a small boulder.

The shiny glint of metal caught his eye, and he lowered himself behind the rock for cover, and fired. A second later, a loud *thunk* followed.

Had he killed the jerk?

His heart hammering, he crept closer, but suddenly the crunch of leaves crackled behind him. He turned a millisecond too late and saw the gun coming down toward him. The butt of the weapon slammed against his temple, and he swayed with the force.

He fired a shot before he went down and tried to see the man's face, but he missed the shot, and a blow to his gut made his knees buckle.

He tasted dirt and clawed for his gun, but it skidded across the ground a foot away from him. The shooter kicked it over by a pile of rocks, then brought his foot down and stomped on Maddox's hand. Pain ricocheted through his fingers and arm, and he thought he heard the bones in his fingers cracking.

Dammit. He had to get up. Then he felt the barrel of the gun against the back of his head, and he froze.

Dear God, if the man shot him, he couldn't save Rose...

TIME SEEMED TO stand still for Rose.

Maddox was outside, and someone was shooting at him this time. She couldn't hide out. She had to save him.

She searched the room frantically for a weapon, anything to protect herself, but her room and her parents' room held nothing helpful.

Outside, another shot fired, then the sound of the door screeching open filled the air. She waited to hear Maddox's voice, but he didn't call out.

Terrified he'd been shot, she ran for her parents' closet. Maybe there was something she could use as a weapon inside.

She ducked inside the closet and gripped the umbrella, the hint of mothballs almost making her choke. For a moment, memories launched her back to the night her parents were murdered.

This was the closet where she'd hidden years ago, where she'd peeked out and seen the man shoot her mother.

Footsteps shuffled outside the door. She held her breath, praying Maddox had overcome the shooter, but icy terror ripped through her as the man's voice called her name. "Rose?"

Whose voice was that?

"Rose...Rose, it's over. Come out now."

Where was Maddox?

Clenching the umbrella with a white-knuckled grip, she waited, listening to his footsteps as he combed through the house.

Suddenly the footsteps halted. The house grew eerily quiet. The wind whistled, then the voice again. "Rose...I know where you are now."

Trembling, she blinked back tears. He didn't sound as if he was here to help her. He sounded...like the man who'd called her the night she'd escaped Thad.

She looked down at the floor and saw a shadow in front of the door. He was outside the closet.

He jiggled the doorknob, and she tried to hold it shut, but he yanked it open. Light seeped through the cracks, just enough for her to see the outline of his face.

Except for a brief second, that face was much younger. It was the boy she'd seen outside the window in the swing.

The one she'd played with as a child.

"This is where you always liked to hide," he said. "You were in there that night, weren't you?"

"Carl," she rasped. Carl Redding. "You...were my friend." Shock strained her lungs. "And your father...he was my father's friend."

Only...now she remembered. She'd thought their parents were friends. But something had changed, they'd argued that night.

Then he'd shot her parents...

MADDOX STIRRED FROM UNCONSCIOUSNESS, his head throbbing, dirt clogging his throat. He blinked to clear his vision and realized he was lying facedown.

Where the hell was he?

He mentally retraced the last few minutes before he'd lost consciousness. He'd been outside Rose's house near the woods...then someone had shot at him.

Panic seized him as the truth dawned. *Dammit*, the shooter had gotten the best of him. And now he was tied up on the floor of some...shed.

Did the shooter have Rose now?

He lifted his head and searched the darkness. His pulse pounded at the sight of a body in the corner. He watched to see if the man moved, but judging from the stench emanating from him, he was dead.

Adrenaline surged through him, and he tried to push himself up, but his hands were bound behind his back, his feet tied. His head throbbed, and he spit blood from where he must have bitten his tongue when he was attacked.

He had to get to Rose.

He visually scanned the dark space, searching for an escape route. Old gardening tools had been jammed to one side. A workbench occupied another corner. A hoe stood by the door.

If he could get to that door, maybe he could get out and save Rose.

He looked around in search of his phone or gun, but they were nowhere to be seen.

Frustration fueled his anger, and he used his elbows to drag himself across the floor. Wood splintered and cracked beneath him as his weight pressed against the loose boards, but he inched forward until he reached the hoe. Beside it, he spotted a small rake, and twisted sideways in an attempt to use it like a knife to cut the ropes on his hands.

He tried sawing back and forth, but the ropes were thick, the blade of the rake dull. He twisted and turned his hands, yanking at the ropes, but they were tied so tightly he couldn't budge the knot.

The need to hurry gnawed at him as he searched for another tool to free himself. He didn't see anything, so he decided to crawl over to the dead man. If he hadn't been here long, maybe he had a phone or something sharp in his pocket.

Of course if he had, he probably would have used it to escape himself.

Still, he dragged himself toward the body, forcing himself to breathe out so he wouldn't gag, as the stench of death grew stronger.

Outside, a scream pierced the air.

Maddox froze, his blood turning cold.

Rose...

God, what was that maniac doing to her?

He moved as quickly as he could, gritting his teeth at the foul odor. The whites of the man's eyes bugled in the dark, and blood had dried on his mouth.

Good God. It was Marshal Norton.

Maddox twisted sideways, determined to search his pocket, but his hand touched something sticky—more blood?

Another scream from outside sent his heart into panic mode.

The scent of smoke wafted through the shed, and he heard wood crackling. Smoke seeped through the cracks and filled the shed, and Maddox cursed.

If he didn't get untied, he was going to burn in here alive.

Then Rose would be at the mercy of the man who wanted her dead...

ROSE CRIED OUT in horror as Carl spread gas along the shed and lit a match. He'd already burned down her house. Killed the Worthingtons.

And her parents...no, his father had done that....

She struggled with the ropes binding her arms and feet as he shoved her in the backseat of the sedan.

"You can't just leave him here to die," Rose shouted. "And there's a marshal after you. He'll figure out who you are."

A sinister laugh rumbled from him. "That marshal won't be a problem anymore," he said. "He's in there with your cowboy cop."

Horror washed over Rose at his words and the flames sprouting up at the door to the shed. If Maddox didn't die of smoke inhalation first, he'd burn to death.

"You hired Thad to kill me? What was your connection to him?"

Carl made a low sound in his throat. "We met in the

service and kept in touch." A sinister smile tugged at his mouth. "Thad was a natural sniper. Amazing how he enjoyed the work when I couldn't wait to get out."

"You rescued him after I shot him," Rose said, piecing together the facts. "You helped clean up the cabin and got him medical care, didn't you?"

Carl shrugged. "What else could I do? He hadn't finished the job."

Rose's head reeled. "And your father had connections to get him treated for the gunshot wound?"

"Actually I took care of it," Carl said. "I was a medic in the military."

"If you saved people then, how can you kill me now?"

His eyes narrowed, turmoil darkening them. "It's not what I wanted, Rose. But my family will lose everything if I don't." He stiffened. "In the military, I was taught to do what I had to do to protect my country. And my country is my family."

She would admire his loyalty if it wasn't so misplaced. "Please, Carl, let me go."

"I can't do that, Rose." He reached for her again, but she lunged toward the door to jump out.

He raised the pistol and whipped her across the face. Pain slammed into her jaw and screamed through her head, and she fell backward into the seat.

Back into the dark.

Some time later Rose woke to the rumbling of the car. It bounced over a rut, gravel churning, then she slid sideways as they swerved to the right and the car barreled up a hill.

She had no idea how long they'd been traveling or where they were.

Fear choked her. Though she remembered seeing Carl light the shed on fire, was it possible Maddox had escaped? Or was he...dead?

The car screeched to a stop, and she pitched forward and

nearly fell to the floor, but caught herself with her feet. Before she could sit up, Carl swung the back door open and dragged her out of the car. She kicked and struggled, but he shook her hard.

"There's no use fighting, Rose. Cooperate and I might let you live."

"Like you did the Worthingtons?"

"All they had to do was tell me where the money was."

"What money?" Rose cried.

"The money they stole from my father."

Rose's pulse stuttered. "I don't believe you."

Carl grabbed her arm and yanked her toward a rustic-looking cabin nestled in the woods by the river. Deep pockets of rocks and boulders made up the rugged landscape, hiding the location.

He shoved her forward, pushing her over the rugged terrain until they reached the cabin, then he forced her inside. Rose expected it to be completely rustic inside, but the place actually looked nice, homey, lived-in.

Not a place to die at the hands of a cold-blooded killer.

He shoved her onto the floor by the fireplace.

Adrenaline spiked her anger. "Why didn't you just leave me there to die with Maddox?"

"Because you know too much. You saw my father that night with your parents."

"He shot them. But I don't understand why."

"It was your father's fault." Carl began to pace in front of the fireplace, his face tight with agitation.

"How was it *his* fault?"

Carl glared at her. "My father was the head of a drug company. Your dad worked for him."

That part of the past was a blur. Then again, she'd been only four at the time, Carl older, maybe eight.

"What happened?"

Carl slumped onto the couch to face her, his hand still

clenching the gun. "My father patented a new drug they'd been testing for mood disorders, but your father found flaws in the study. Hell, he was an accountant. He wasn't supposed to look into the research at all. The company was about to go public with this new drug, and Dad would have lost a fortune if your father had questioned it."

"So your dad was going to sell a drug under false pretenses?" Rose said, not bothering to hide the derision from her voice.

"Dad planned to rectify the problems after the deal went through, but your father threatened to blow the whistle. So my father offered your dad a big payout to keep quiet."

Nausea bubbled in Rose's throat. "My father took a bribe to keep quiet?"

"It was a lot of money," Carl said. "I guess he wanted to be able to take care of you and your mother."

"If my dad took the money, why did your father kill him?"

Carl vaulted to his feet, then scraped a hand through his hair, agitated. "What difference does it make now?"

"You and your father destroyed my life," Rose said. "At least I deserve to know the whole story before I die."

Chapter Twenty-Two

Maddox crawled toward the door, then managed to get up on his knees and push against it with his body, hoping to open it. But it didn't budge.

He staggered as smoke choked him, but mustered up all his strength and rammed the door with his shoulder. The wood cracked, but felt hot.

Dammit, the boards were rotting and would catch fast. Was there another way out?

He shuffled toward the back, but the ropes around his feet made him clumsy and he fell. Cursing, he shoved himself back up to his feet and made it a little farther, when the front side of the shed erupted into flames.

Knowing he needed to hurry, he scooted as fast as he could, but when he managed to reach the wall, he didn't see another door.

Frustration made him twist and jerk at the ropes, but nothing worked, and the smoke was growing thicker, the smell of burning wood becoming stronger as heat seared his skin.

Rose's sweet face the night before when they'd made love taunted him. She was too beautiful to die.

Rage churned through him, and he banged against a loose board in the wall. He used his shoulder to ram it over and over until the wood splintered. He slammed it again, hitting it with as much force as he could, then again until he busted through the wood.

Loose boards scratched his face as he dove to the ground below, and he rolled across the ground to put some distance between him and the shed. Flames shot from the structure and smoke curled into the sky.

The sound of a motor rumbling broke into the night, then headlights dotted the dirt. A van barreled over the terrain and roared to a stop.

Hoberman and the CSI team piled out. Relieved to see them, Maddox crawled to his knees and yelled Hoberman's name. "I'm over here!"

The sound of wood burning and popping filled the air, drowning out his voice.

He staggered as he tried to stand and shuffled to the right in the clearing so Hoberman could see him. "Over here! Untie me!"

Hoberman jogged toward him. "What happened?"

"Marshal Norton is dead inside. Another man ambushed us. He took Rose. We have to hurry!"

Hoberman made quick work of untying the ropes. "Where were they going?"

"I don't know." Maddox gestured toward the burning shed. "Marshal Norton's body is in there." Maddox headed back toward the building. "I've got to get him out."

"Wait, McCullen, a fire engine is on its way."

But Maddox ran toward the shed and tore through the back. Flames were spreading along the floor toward the body, but he yanked the man by the feet and dragged him to the edge, where he'd splintered the wood. Hoberman rushed to help him, and they hauled the man through the hole in the wall and dragged him near the river.

The wail of a siren screamed, coming closer, and one of Hoberman's team approached them. "They'll work on the fire. What do you want us to do?"

Maddox wiped sweat and soot from his face with his sleeve. "This is the house where Rose lived until she was four. Her parents were shot inside. I need you to process it for prints, DNA, whatever forensics you can find. Everything that's happened is connected to those murders."

"We'll get right on it." The team retrieved their crime kits and strode toward the old house.

Maddox kneeled beside the body. "I'm going to call the Marshals Service and see what I can find out. Norton must have stumbled on to the truth, and the killer got worried he was going to get caught."

He just wished to hell he knew what that truth was.

Maybe someone at the Marshals Service did.

He punched the number, identified himself and explained that he'd found Marshal Norton dead. "It's important I talk to someone who knows about the case he was working on," Maddox said. "The suspect has taken a hostage. Finding him is the only way to save the woman's life."

"IT WAS YOUR mother's fault," Carl told Rose.

Rose glared at him. "You're blaming my *mother* because your father was a liar and planned to cheat people."

"I told you my father was going to fix the problem with the drug. But your mother found out about the deal and convinced your father to go to the police. When Dad confronted him, they fought and the gun went off. Your mother tried to break it up, and they fought, too, and…he shot her."

Carl's voice cracked. "Dad didn't go there to kill them. He only wanted to stop them from ruining the deal."

"It doesn't justify murder," Rose said, seething.

Carl threw his hands up, his voice angry. "I told you it was an accident."

"I saw him yank my mother by the hair and put the gun to her head," Rose shouted. "That was no accident. And he would have killed me if he'd found me. But the police showed up and saved me, and then the Worthingtons kidnapped me and ran."

"Yeah, he was on their tail, but they had an accident and you all wound up in the hospital. With all the staff around, he couldn't get near you."

Norton had mentioned the accident. She rubbed the scar again. That was when she'd gotten the scar.

"So your father has been looking for them ever since?"

"At first he did, but when they didn't come forward and you didn't remember, he let it go. He thought it was all right."

Rose twisted, sickened by what he was saying. They had played together as children yet she didn't know this man. "So why come after me now?"

Carl paced again, one hand running back and forth over his neck, the other waving the gun. "Because Dad is about to be honored with a humanitarian award for his work."

Reality dawned, ugly and cold. "And he was afraid I'd recognize him and destroy his career."

"He did good work," Carl shouted. "He fixed the problems with that original drug and took care of the side effects."

"And paid anyone who'd suffered from the side effects to keep quiet?" Rose asked.

Carl shrugged. "I told you he did good things. He shouldn't have to pay for a mistake he made when he was young. But that damned Marshal Norton, he came around asking questions. For some reason, he decided to look into the old case, your parents' case, because that flyer of you on the milk carton surfaced. When he showed up at my father's asking questions, he got nervous. If the marshal convinced the Worthingtons to come forward with the truth, he would have been exposed."

"Your father ruined all our lives—mine, my parents', the Worthingtons'—because of his lies and greed," Rose cried. "He committed murder, and now you have blood on your hands. The blood of that marshal, and the Worthingtons." *And maybe Maddox's.*

God, she hoped he wasn't dead...

Carl scrubbed his hand through his hair. "I won't let you or anyone else ruin our family's name and what my father has built."

"Because you're a selfish, greedy bastard," Rose said in disgust. Confusion swirled in her head. "You have plenty of money. So why would you care about the money you claim my father took?"

"Because it links your parents' murder back to my father. If that marshal found that out, so could someone else."

"How could they link cash back to him?"

"It wasn't just cash," Carl growled. "Your father had a tape of their conversation. He put the money with that tape for safekeeping, but that night he refused to reveal where he'd hidden it."

Rose couldn't wrap her mind around the fact that her father had practically blackmailed Carl's dad. But if she found that tape she'd have proof that Mr. Redding had murdered her parents.

Carl waved the gun at her again. "Where is it, Rose? I turned that old house inside out searching for it. And it wasn't at the Worthingtons'." He leaned over, hands on his knees, and pushed his face into hers. "Where is it, Rose? Where would your father have hidden it? Did you have a special toy that he could have hidden the tape inside?"

A toy? A vision of her stuffed animals torn apart with the stuffing spilling out flashed back. Had Carl split them open in search of the tape and the money? "If he did, I didn't know anything about it."

"Think," Carl said, his voice shrill.

Pure panic flared in his eyes. If she didn't figure out where he'd hidden it, Carl would kill her.

She swallowed hard. *He'll kill you anyway.*

For all she knew, her father had lied about the tape, had made it up as a precaution. And no telling where he'd stuck that cash. If in fact, he actually had taken it.

She couldn't believe anything Carl said.

Her only hope was to stall. If Maddox was still alive, she had to give him time to find her.

MADDOX SPOKE WITH the head of the US Marshals' office, a man named Stone Hunter, as the crime team processed the homestead and the firefighters extinguished the shed fire. "Yes, we found Marshal Norton dead. And the killer took Rose Worthington hostage." He explained what he knew so far and his suspicions.

"Yes, Norton was investigating the Worthingtons and searching for that little girl on the milk carton. Apparently Norton's uncle was the sheriff who worked the case years ago. He put the little girl in that foster home and never got over the fact that she was kidnapped on his watch. On his deathbed, he asked his nephew to continue looking for her."

"What did Norton find out?"

"Hang on, I'm accessing his files now."

Maddox heard the tapping of keys and silently urged the man to hurry. Every second meant Rose could be closer to death.

"His notes indicate that the little girl's real name was Hailey Hudgens. Her father, Keith, worked for a pharmaceutical company owned by Bill Redding."

"*The* Bill Redding of Redding Pharmaceuticals?"

"One and the same," Hunter said. "Norton scribbled notes that he suspected Hudgens discovered Redding falsified data regarding drug testing to push FDA approval and made a fortune."

"But Norton said Rose's birth parents and the Worthingtons were involved in money laundering?"

"That was a theory early on when the couple went missing, but his notes here say he didn't believe it. That he suspected Redding murdered the Hudgenses to keep them quiet about the pharmaceutical."

"The Worthingtons, aka Millie and Lloyd Curtain, were friends of the Hudgenses. They took the little girl and went into hiding, because she witnessed the murder and could identify Redding?" Maddox said.

"That's what Norton believed."

"So they were protecting her?"

"Yes."

"When Norton began digging into the old case, Redding must have panicked and hired someone to kill Rose," Maddox said.

"That makes sense," Hunter said. "And explains how Thad Thoreau got involved."

"The man who assaulted me and kidnapped Rose is too young to be Redding," Maddox said. "He probably hired him. Do you have an address for Redding?"

More keys clicking, then Hunter replied, "Yes. Oh, and according to this, Redding has a son named Carl. I'll text you his photo now."

Maddox's phone dinged with the incoming text, and he cursed as he looked at the picture. "*Dammit*, Rose mentioned that she overheard Thad talking to a man named Carl. Carl must have Rose now."

Hunter scowled. "I'll send men to Redding's office and home."

"Good, but the son wouldn't take her there."

"Maybe not, but we can pressure Redding to tell us where he'd go."

"Good point. Did Redding own any property away from town? A vacation home or cabin somewhere remote?"

"Let me look." A tense minute passed, then Hunter spoke again. "Yes. I'll text you the GPS coordinates now."

"Thanks." Maddox joined Hoberman again, and quickly relayed what he'd learned. "Call me if you find something," he yelled as he jogged toward his car.

He flipped on his siren, pressed the accelerator and roared away. According to his GPS, the place was about thirty miles away.

"Hang on, Rose," he whispered. "I'm coming."

ROSE'S MIND RACED for a way to stall Carl. But he was pacing, his movements agitated, his words becoming incoherent.

"How can you do this to me? We played together when we were children." She searched his face for any semblance of the kind boy she'd once known. "You pushed me in the tire swing. I remember that now. And we played hide-and-seek and roasted marshmallows on that old metal rim that my father used as a grill."

Carl paused, his eyes wild with anger and panic. "Don't you see? I can't stop now. It's too late."

"You don't have to kill me," Rose said. "Is that what your father wanted? For you to become a murderer?"

"My father wanted to build an empire and help people," Carl shouted. "And he did, but your father was going to ruin it."

"Just because they messed up doesn't mean we have to," Rose argued. "You can stop it now, Carl. Stop the violence and prove that you're a good man."

Carl fisted his hands and shook them in the air, sweat beading on his skin. "You don't understand. It's too late."

"No, it's not too late. It's never too late to do the right thing."

His eyes flared with indecision, regret. But he continued pacing, his hand tightening around the gun. "Just tell me where the tape is."

"I told you, I don't know anything about money or a tape."

He grabbed her by her hair and shook her. "Think, Rose!"

A sob caught in her throat. "I'm sorry, Carl, but you're wrong. The Worthingtons lived a meager life, we didn't have much, they never bought things. They didn't have any money."

He yanked her up by her hair and dragged her toward the door. "Then I've got no use for you."

"Wait!" she cried. "Don't do this, Carl, please."

She tried to elbow him, but he slammed the gun at her temple again and pain ripped through her head. She swayed, dizzy and nauseated, then he dragged her outside.

Terrified, she dug her heels in, but he yanked her so hard her knees buckled, then he hauled her across the ground. Her legs and arms scraped dry brush, gravel digging into her sides.

But he dragged her toward the river, his rage out of control, then shoved her facedown into the water.

She held her breath, but mud and water seeped into her nose and she gagged. He jammed his foot on her back to hold her down, and pushed her deeper. She lost her breath and began to choke.

Chapter Twenty-Three

Maddox spotted the sedan parked by the cabin and prayed he wasn't too late. But that car meant Carl had brought Rose here.

He gripped his gun at the ready, pulled to a stop and jumped out. He headed toward the house, trying not to alert the man that he'd arrived, as he scanned the property and house for activity.

A light burned in the front room.

He eased up to the window and peered inside, but he didn't see anyone. A noise from the back jarred him, and he hurried around the side of the cabin, braced to fire.

His heart stopped when he spotted the outline of a man.

And Rose—*dear God*, she was on her knees and the man was holding her down in the water. The bastard was going to drown her.

Maddox inched closer until he stood less than a foot away, then lifted his weapon and aimed it at Carl. "Let her go," he growled. "Or you're a dead man."

Carl pivoted enough to see Maddox and the gun he had shoved in his face. Fear widened his eyes, and he released Rose. She fell face forward in the water like a rag doll.

"Rose!" Maddox kept the gun trained on Carl, and hurried to drag her from the river. But Carl lunged toward him, swung his arm up and knocked at his gun hand. The gun fired into the air, and the two men fought for it.

Maddox gripped it with all his might, and slammed his fist into Carl's gut. Carl grunted but fought back, and the two of them traded blows. A hard one to the solar plexus sent Maddox staggering for a moment, and Carl jumped him.

They went down in a tangle, but rage fueled Maddox, and he bucked the man off him and rolled him to his belly. He glanced sideways for the gun but didn't see it. *Dammit*. It had fallen between some rocks.

Carl shoved him, but Maddox balled his hand into a fist and punched him in the face. Blood spurted from Carl's nose and he spit out a curse, but an image of the man holding Rose's face in the water taunted him, and Maddox punched him again.

Carl's head lolled to the side, but fury made Maddox punch him again and again until he lay limp.

Finally a noise behind him brought him back to reality. *Rose...*

God...

He jumped off Carl and ran toward her. She was struggling to push herself up from the water, but the current was about to drag her away. He raced into the edge of the river, took her shoulders and lifted her head above water. She coughed and he picked her up, carried her to the embankment and laid her in the grass.

"Rose, it's me, you're okay." He quickly untied her hands, then raked her wet hair from her face and felt for a pulse, but it was weak and thready. She was also shivering from the elements. Worried about hypothermia, he jerked off his jacket and wrapped it around her. Scratches marked her face from the rocks but thankfully, there was no gunshot wound.

He tilted her head back and checked her airway, then

crossed his hands and pressed gently on her chest. Once. Twice. Seconds later, she coughed and began to spit water. He rolled her sideways, holding her head while she coughed up the murky river water.

He stroked her face, grateful when she opened her eyes. They looked weak, strained, frightened, but when she saw him, a relieved breath rushed from her chest. "Maddox?"

"I've got you," he said in a hoarse whisper.

She tried to nod, but was obviously too weak. A noise sounded behind him. Brush rustling. He swung around and saw Carl crawling toward his gun.

Maddox lurched up, darted to the rocks where his gun had fallen, snatched his weapon and aimed it. Carl swung his arm around and fired at Maddox, but Maddox dodged the bullet and fired back.

His bullet pierced Carl's chest. Carl's eyes widened in shock as he sank like a rock. Maddox gripped his gun and strode toward the man, keeping his eyes on him in case he rallied. But when he reached him, Carl lay still, his lips parted in shock, his eyes wide in death.

Still, Maddox checked for a pulse. Nothing.

Relieved, he grabbed the bastard's gun and jammed it in the waistband of his pants, then hurried back to Rose. Grateful she was alive, he pulled her into his arms and held her as he called for an ambulance.

THE NEXT FEW HOURS passed in a blur for Rose. She was so exhausted from her near death that she allowed the medics to transport her to the hospital for rest and observation.

Maddox assured her he'd meet her at the hospital after he moved Carl's body to the morgue.

She slept for what seemed like hours, her dreams riddled with nightmares of Carl trying to drown her. When she woke up, morning light poured through the window, but she could still taste the stench of the muddy river water.

She rubbed her eyes and propped herself against the pillows, then spotted Maddox in the chair in the corner, his head lolled to the side in sleep. *When had he come in?*

Hating to wake him when she had no idea how long he'd been asleep, she slid from bed, washed her face and brushed her teeth with the toiletry set the nurse had left. One look in the mirror and she gasped at her disheveled appearance. Her hair was still streaked with dirt and mud. Desperate to wash off the stench of the night before, she showered and put on a clean hospital gown that she found folded on the shelf by the sink. She vaguely remembered the nurse telling her she'd leave it for her when she felt up to a bath. Then she combed her damp hair and tiptoed back to bed.

She was alive and the danger to her was over. She wanted to go home.

Only—she had no home. Carl and Thad had taken that from her, like they'd taken everything else.

Where would she go? Maybe she could stay in the back room at Vintage Treasures.

She pulled the covers up over her, contemplating calling the nurse to be discharged. Maddox stirred, then looked at her from the chair. His jaw was dark with stubble, his eyes grim.

"How do you feel, Rose?"

She swallowed back the emotions his gruff voice stirred. "Better now I showered."

A muscle ticked in his jaw, and she realized he was looking at the bruises on her neck and face. Self-consciously she rubbed her neck.

"Carl's body is at the morgue. We arrested his father last night."

A sigh of relief escaped her. "Did he confess to killing my parents?"

Maddox gave a noncommittal shrug. "He lawyered up.

But the CSI team that searched and processed your parents' house found his prints there. And…they found the tape your father had recorded. Your father never took money from him, Rose. He turned it down flat. That's the reason Redding killed him."

Relief flooded Rose At least her parents had been honest, good people. "Where did they find the tape?"

"In the little jewelry box in your room."

"The ballerina music box?"

He nodded. "CSI hunted everywhere in the house for a secret hiding place. Then I remembered how much your mother loved the music boxes she collected and told them to search for a music box. The only one in the house was—"

"The pink one I had as a child."

"Right. Your father had hidden a key to a safety deposit box under the bottom." He removed a small envelope from inside his jacket and handed it to her. "These were also tucked inside."

Rose took the envelope and opened it, tears swelling in her eyes at the sight of the handful of photographs tucked inside—pictures of her as a baby and a little child with her birth parents. They were holding her, loving her, celebrating Christmases and birthdays and having a picnic at the park.

She wiped at the tears and offered Maddox a grateful look. "Thank you so much for these, Maddox."

"You're welcome." He paused. "There's something else."

What more could there be?

"Trina Fields…I know you thought she worked with Thad Thoreau, but that's not exactly the story."

The sense of betrayal she'd felt with Trina returned to dig at her gut.

"Then what is the story?"

"She should be the one to explain."

Rose frowned, confused. "Why? If she helped Thoreau—"

"Trust me, you're going to want to hear her side." Maddox stood. "Are you up for it now? She's awake and anxious to talk to you."

Rose swallowed hard. "Fine."

"I'll call the nurse for a wheelchair."

"I don't need a chair, Maddox, I can walk." She swung her legs over the side of the bed, making sure the gown was tied in place, then allowed him to hold her arm as they walked down the hall to Trina's room.

She took a deep breath when she entered, a mixture of hurt and curiosity crowding her chest as Trina looked up at her with a tentative smile.

Maddox grabbed the chair from the corner and situated it by Trina's bed. "Sit down, Rose."

Her legs felt weak, and she sank into the chair and knotted her hands.

"I'll leave you two alone to talk."

She started to protest, to tell Maddox she needed him, but bit back the words. Now she was safe, she had to learn to stand on her own again. Maddox had his own problems.

"Thank you for coming, Rose," Trina said softly.

Rose gripped the edge of the chair with her fingers, ready to bolt any second. "Maddox said you wanted to explain."

Trina pushed herself to a sitting position, wincing as she settled the blanket in place. She was obviously in pain from the surgery.

"I'm sorry for the way things happened," Trina said. "But I want you to know the truth."

"You helped Thad Thoreau find me and…you both lied to me."

"He used me," Trina said. "I had no idea he wanted to hurt you, Rose. You have to believe me when I say that. *I* would never hurt you."

"But you did by helping him."

"That wasn't my intent. You have no idea how sorry I am. How much I regret trusting him."

Rose worried her bottom lip with her teeth. "What do you mean, he used you?"

Trina ran a hand through her short hair, spiking the ends. For a moment, she looked young and vulnerable. "I'm adopted," she began. "My adopted parents were great, and I loved them. But they were killed in a car accident a few months ago, and I decided to search for my birth family, for any relatives I might have. Thad told me he worked for an agency that helped adopted children find their families. He agreed to help me search."

Rose wrinkled her forehead, confused. "But he told me he worked for an energy company."

"I know. He used that as a cover story to get to know you."

"I still don't understand."

"Just bear with me. A couple of months after I hired him, he called and told me to come to Pistol Whip, that he'd found something. So I came here and applied for a job at Vintage Treasures." Trina worried her bottom lip with her teeth. "At first, I was nervous. I didn't tell you what I was doing, because I wanted to make sure it was true."

Rose was still having trouble following her. "Make sure what was true?"

Trina wet her lips with her tongue.

"What do you remember about your birth mother?" Trina asked.

Rose toyed with the hem of her hospital gown. "Not much, just that she liked music boxes, and she let me crawl in bed with her at night when I was scared, and she'd sing to me."

Trina picked at a broken fingernail. "You don't remember that she was pregnant when she died?"

Rose gasped, struggling to recall details of her mother's face. Her body. But she'd been so little at the time...

"In fact, she was almost nine months pregnant," Trina said. "Apparently she delivered the baby right before she died. The man who killed her took that infant and left it at a church nearby."

Rose massaged the scar at her temple. "That means I have a sister or a brother?"

Trina reached out her hand. "A sister, Rose. The baby girl that was born that night was me."

MADDOX WATCHED ROSE and Trina through the window of the hospital room door, relieved, because in spite of everything she'd undergone, Rose wasn't alone.

His job was done.

So why was he so reluctant to leave?

Because Rose's home had been destroyed, and she had no place to go.

That's not true, he reminded himself. Now she had a sister, one she needed to get to know better. Rose would probably want to stay with her.

His phone buzzed, and he checked the number. Home.

His chest clenched as fear gripped him. Was his father okay?

He inhaled a deep breath and pressed Connect. "Mama Mary?"

"Yeah, Maddox. It's me. You won't believe it, but Brett just showed up at the ranch."

"He's there now?"

"Yep. In the kitchen having some of my biscuits and gravy. Eatin' like he hasn't eaten in days."

Maddox gritted his teeth. Brett was probably already charming Mama Mary. She had a soft spot for his little-boy act and fell for his compliments as if she was a schoolgirl.

"Has he seen Dad yet?"

"No, he's stalling, of course. I thought you might want to be here when he does."

Dammit, his father wanted to see the brothers all together again. But could they tolerate being in the same room without tearing each other apart?

Chapter Twenty-Four

Rose stared at Trina in shock. "My sister?"

"Yes," Trina said with a hopeful smile. "I couldn't believe it at first, either. But I actually took a strand of hair from your hairbrush and sent it away to have the DNA checked, and it was a match for mine."

"Oh, my goodness," Rose said. "All this time I had no idea."

"I wasn't sure how much you knew," Trina said. "It took me a while to put all the pieces together, too. To find out who'd adopted you. Then Thad told me you'd been kidnapped and that you might not remember what happened, so I decided to get to know you before I told you my story."

"You didn't think it was strange that Thad started a romance with me, that he proposed?"

Regret tugged at Trina's face. "I thought he fell in love with you. I really did." Her eyes begged for forgiveness. "I mean, how could he not? You're beautiful and strong and smart. You started your own business. I…I wanted to be like you. And…" Her voice cracked. "I was so glad to find you, to know that I wasn't alone anymore, and I wanted you to be happy. I thought he loved you."

Now Rose understood what Trina meant about Thad using her.

"I'm sorry for the way things happened," Trina said. "But I want us to be friends."

Tears burned the backs of Rose's eyelids. She'd always felt as if she didn't belong with the Worthingtons, hadn't understood them. Then she'd lost them and felt all alone.

Now she had a sister. A real family.

She reached out and took Trina's hand in hers. "I'm glad you found me, Trina. I want us to be friends, too."

She hugged Trina, and they both wiped at tears as Rose began to tell her the few things she remembered about their mother and father, and what she'd learned from Carl about the night they were murdered.

MADDOX STEELED HIMSELF against seeing his brothers again. It had been ages since they'd been home. Longer since they'd gotten along.

They'd all grown up. Matured.

Had time changed things?

It didn't matter. His brothers had their own lives. They'd probably stay long enough to see their father, then they'd leave again, and he'd stay here and run Horseshoe Creek.

Alone.

Only the idea of completely being alone again gave him an unsettling feeling, and an image of Rose appeared in his mind. Beautiful, sweet, loving, strong Rose.

The first woman who had ever touched his heart.

His gaze caught sight of the black pickup with the license plate that read Texas, and he knew it belonged to Brett. A black Range Rover was parked beside it, tag from Montana.

Had to be Ray.

Maddox ran his hand over his face as he parked and walked up to the porch, his rough stubble a reminder that he hadn't been home the night before. He needed a shower and a shave and some strong coffee.

But when he opened the door, tension vibrated in the air. His brothers were home. His father was dying.

And he…wanted Rose.

Mama Mary met him with a cup of coffee and gave him a hug. "You okay, Mr. Maddox? I know you were gone all night."

"I'm fine. I just need to clean up."

"How's Miss Rose?"

"We found the man who tried to kill her. She'll be okay now," Maddox said, thinking of the way he'd left her with Trina. Those two would need time to get to know each other, to bond and share their grief.

For all he knew, they might even decide to move away from Pistol Whip. He couldn't blame them if they wanted to leave the bad memories behind.

Voices echoed from the kitchen, and he stepped inside. Brett and Ray were sitting at the table devouring Mama Mary's huckleberry pie.

The years had added character and lines to both their faces. He'd seen photos of Brett from the rodeo circuit. He'd put on muscle, his nose had been broken at least twice, and he wore his hair shaggy and a little too long, but women were always swarming all over him. That boyish, mischievous glint still flickered in his eyes, though, as if he was about to crack a joke or flirt with some woman in a bar.

Ray hadn't changed much, either. Bronzed skin, wide shoulders, hard jaw. A few lines around his dark eyes, eyes that looked black with anger and distrust, just as they always had.

"Now, boys," Mama Mary said. "Your daddy had a rough night. He's anxious to see you, so I guess you'd best get to it."

An awkwardness stretched between the brothers, but Maddox didn't bother to try to smooth it over. His brothers were here for one reason, and none of them liked it.

"I'll go first," Brett said, although his tone suggested he'd rather be chased by a bull.

Maddox nodded, and Brett headed to the hall and up the stairs. Ray and he followed and waited outside the bedroom door, the seconds ticking by with unspoken tension.

"Mama Mary said you were working an investigation," Ray finally said.

Maddox shrugged. "Yeah. It's over now, though." *And so was his time with Rose.*

Although that thought nearly smothered him with longing.

"I'm a PI now," Ray revealed, surprising Maddox by offering the information.

Maddox simply grunted. "Thanks for coming back."

Another canyon of silence fell between them, then the door opened and Brett stepped out. His head was down, his expression grim. He bypassed them, then jogged down the steps and slammed the front door.

Ray gave Maddox a sharp look as if to say, "See, this was a mistake." Resigned, though, he ducked inside the bedroom and shut the door.

Maddox paced the hallway, anxiety knotting his shoulders as he waited. What was his father saying to Ray? What was Ray saying to him?

Time dragged by, slow and torturous, then suddenly the door opened and Ray yelled for him.

"Get in here, Maddox."

Maddox raced inside and saw his father gasping for air. "Call the doctor!"

He ran to his father's bed and tried to adjust the oxygen mask while Ray snatched his phone and hurried into the hall to make the call.

His father motioned for him to lean close. Maddox's heart hammered as he did.

"Take care of them, but take care of yourself, too," his father rasped.

"Dad—"

His father lifted a frail hand and gestured toward the dresser. "Your mother's engagement ring is in that box in the drawer. She wanted you to have it, to give it to the woman you love."

Maddox's eyes stung with emotions, but he sank into the chair beside his father, and gripped his hand.

"Promise me, Maddox," his father murmured. "That you'll find a wife and be happy."

Maddox swallowed hard. "I promise, Dad."

A second later, his father closed his eyes and whispered good-bye.

Epilogue

Three days later

ROSE HAD STAYED with Trina while her sister recovered and shared the few photographs Maddox had found for her of their parents.

She still could hardly believe it—she had a sister.

But it was time she looked for another place to live. Her rental house was in ruins, and Trina's apartment was too small for both of them.

She had to put the past behind her. Forget the violence that had changed the course of her life.

She stepped into the coffee shop and ordered a sandwich and tea. Several women at the table by the counter were talking.

"So sad that Joe McCullen passed," one of the women said. "His funeral is at two this afternoon."

"He was a good man," a gray-haired woman in a pink dress said. "I bet the church will be packed."

"I feel for his son Maddox," another lady said. "He reminds me of Joe."

"Those other two McCullen boys are back. Guess they'll be at the service."

Rose paid for her food and hurried out to her car. She

remembered the grief in Maddox's voice when he'd mentioned that his father was ill. He'd also admitted he and his brothers didn't get along.

How was he handling the situation?

Her heart ached for him. She'd missed him the last few days, had wanted to see him. Not because she was afraid for her life anymore.

Because she was in love with the man.

But she'd made mistakes before, and she'd been terrified of admitting her feelings for him.

She returned to her store to eat, then spent the next hour organizing a display of antique dishes she'd found at a local estate sale, but her mind kept straying to Maddox and the grief he must be feeling.

She had to be there for him.

The parking lot of the church was packed when she arrived. She slipped inside and spotted Mama Mary on a pew behind Maddox and two dark-haired men who resembled Maddox. They must be Brett and Ray.

Maddox sat ramrod-straight, his head high, but that muscle was ticking in his jaw. He was in pain but he was desperately trying to be strong.

Compassion for him filled her. She understood the anguish of losing family.

She tiptoed to the pew and sat down beside Mama Mary, who was knotting a handkerchief in her hands. The sweet woman looked up at Rose, took her hand and squeezed it, then murmured, "Thanks for coming."

The service began, and a tall slender woman sang "Amazing Grace," then the preacher read a scripture and gave a eulogy that had several women in the audience sniffling. Mama Mary broke down, and Rose curved her arm around her and soothed her.

The rest of the service passed in a blur. The pallbearers carried the casket outside, and the family and friends followed to the graveyard. Gray clouds hovered in the sky, threatening rain, and the wind stirred dead leaves on the ground.

As they lowered the casket, Maddox pinched the bridge of his nose and looked away. Rose couldn't help herself.

She tiptoed up behind him and laid her hand on his shoulder. How many times had he comforted her during the last few days?

He glanced up and saw her, and the pain in his eyes tore at her. She squeezed his arm, and he took her hand and gripped it, his shoulders shaking with silent sorrow as Mama Mary dropped rose petals on the grave.

As the service ended, neighbors and friends surrounded the boys to offer condolences.

"I'm so sorry, Maddox." She kissed him on the cheek, then whispered goodbye and left him with his brothers.

MADDOX FORCED HIMSELF to go through the motions of shaking hands with neighbors and people in the community who'd known his father. It felt good to hear stories from his father's friends, people who'd liked and admired him.

Mama Mary lined all the food people brought on the kitchen counter and neighbors dropped by to share stories about Joe and feed their grief with casseroles. Brett and Ray shook hands and accepted regrets, although the tension between them was palpable. But they'd come to a silent agreement that they wouldn't air differences or discuss the future today.

Finally everyone left, Mama Mary packed the food in the fridge and they were alone.

Maddox poured himself a whiskey and offered his brothers one. When they all had drinks, he cleared his throat. "I don't know what you two have planned, but Dad's lawyer wants us to meet for the reading of the will."

"Why?" Ray asked. "We all know Dad wanted you to run the ranch."

Maddox sipped his drink, measuring his words. "Dad wanted the three of us to mend fences. If you want part of the ranch, it's yours, too."

Ray shook his drink in his hand, the ice clinking. "I'll stay for the reading."

Brett downed his whiskey. "Me, too." He set his glass down. "But right now, I think I'll saddle up and take a ride."

Brett always had worked out his problems on a horse.

"I'll be back later." Ray didn't explain where he was going, but he preferred a bar stool at the local honky-tonk when he was upset, so Maddox assumed that was where he was headed.

Maddox stepped outside and looked across the ranch, struck by the silence.

Soon his brothers would leave for good. His father was gone.

And he'd be alone.

Hell, he'd always liked being alone. He had his job. The land, the horses and cattle, the hard work. Horseshoe Creek was home and it had always been enough.

It wasn't enough now.

He wanted more.

His father's words about opening himself up and finding someone special echoed in his head.

He had found someone special. *Rose.*

And he'd fallen in love with her when he was investigating the reason behind her attempted murder.

So what was he going to do about it?

He headed back inside and studied the pictures on the mantel. His mother and father's wedding photo made his chest pound. The frame was broken, and they'd had their share of problems, but on the day they'd married, you could see the love shining in their eyes.

If he confessed his love for Rose, would she reject him? Or could she possibly feel the same way?

She'd made love to him as if she'd wanted him, as if she cared for him. But…she'd been vulnerable and scared then.

He sucked in a sharp breath as an idea struck him. There was something he wanted to give her. Well, two things…

He climbed the steps to his father's room and opened the jewelry box holding his mother's engagement ring. It was a beautiful solitaire diamond in an antique setting.

Remembering his father's words, he stuck it in his pocket.

Too restless to wait, he drove by his office and picked up the little jewelry box with the ballerina that the crime team had taken from her parents' house.

But a case of nerves clenched his stomach as he parked at Trina's apartment, where Rose had been staying. He'd never fallen in love, never done anything this impulsive.

But the thought of being with Rose made him crazy inside.

His heart hammering, he walked up the sidewalk. For a moment, fear clogged his throat and he started to turn around and head home.

But he summoned his courage and rang the bell.

Seconds later, the door opened, and Trina answered. A look of surprise, then concern, darkened her face. "Sheriff, is something wrong? Did Redding get out of jail?"

"No, no, he's still locked up and will be for a long time. I'm here to see Rose."

Trina arched a dark brow. She looked so different from Rose, with her spiked black hair and funky clothes, that it was hard to believe they were sisters.

"I'm afraid she's not here."

Disappointment flooded Maddox. "Do you know where she went?"

Trina shook her head. "She didn't say. She just said not

to wait up on her. That she was looking for a new place to live."

"She's moving?"

Trina nodded. "This place is too small for both of us. I suggested we take the business and relocate to another town. You know, get away from this place where all the bad happened."

He didn't blame them. Rose had been through hell.

But his heart lodged in his throat. If Rose planned to move away, then she must not love him.

And he loved her too much not to let her go.

ROSE HOPED SHE wasn't going to make a fool out of herself.

She was grateful to have found Trina and to have a sister. They'd missed so much of each either's lives that neither of them wanted to miss another moment.

But she missed Maddox, and had never felt more complete than when she was with him.

What she'd thought she'd had with Thad was infatuation based on lies. Maddox was real.

Strong. Caring. Protective. Loving. Devoted to his family. The kind of man she wanted to spend the rest of her life with.

And when Trina suggested relocating, Rose had known she couldn't go. She'd moved all her life. She wanted a home now. A real one, with Maddox.

She parked her car, tucked the gift she'd brought him under her arm and climbed out. But as she walked up to the porch, she noticed his police car was missing.

Disappointment flared inside her, but she decided to leave the gift for him to find when he returned. If he came to thank her personally, it would be a sign that he missed her as well.

Just as she reached the porch, car lights flickered up the

drive and Maddox pulled to a stop. She froze on the steps, the gift box in her hand.

Maddox climbed from the car, a look of surprise on his face. "You're here?"

She offered him a tentative smile although her knees were knocking together. "I have something for you."

He strode toward her, his dark eyes gleaming. "What is it?"

She pushed the box into his hands. "Open it."

Maddox accepted the gift and opened the box, then looked up at her with an eyebrow raised. "It's an antique frame," she said. "I noticed the frame holding your parents' wedding picture was broken, and thought the photograph would look good in here."

A smile twitched at his lips even as turbulent emotions clouded his eyes. "I have something for you, too." He lifted a box from the backseat. "I just came from your house. I was bringing this to you."

Tears pricked at Rose's eyes as she looked in the box. "My ballerina music box."

"I thought you'd want it."

"I do. Thank you."

Rose opened the ballerina box she'd had as a child and smiled as the music began to play and the ballerina danced.

But there was something else inside.

A ring box.

"What's this?" Rose whispered, "Did it belong to my mother?"

"No, it was my mother's."

He took the velvet box from the music box, dropped to one knee in front of her and kissed her hand. "I know you just came off a bad relationship. And that you've just found your sister. And if it's too soon, I understand."

Her breath caught. "Too soon for what?"

He lifted her hand to his lips and kissed her fingers. "For

me to tell you that I need you." He paused, his breath rasping out. "That I miss you. That I want us to be together."

Rose's throat closed with the words she wanted to say.

A heartbeat passed, then he opened the ring box to reveal a beautiful diamond encrusted in an antique setting. "I love you, Rose."

Rose dropped to her knees and squeezed his hands with hers, her heart overflowing with love and happiness and hope. "I love you, too, Maddox."

A grin split his handsome face, and he kissed her tenderly. His dark eyes gleamed with strength and passion and…vulnerability as if he'd been afraid she might not return his feelings.

"Will you marry me, Rose?"

"Yes." Rose threw her arms around his neck and kissed him with all her love.

They'd survived near death.

Now nothing mattered except that she'd finally found a home and a family, and that she and Maddox would be together forever.

* * * * *

THE HEROES OF HORSESHOE CREEK
miniseries continues next month.
Look for McCULLEN'S SECRET SON,
by USA TODAY *bestselling author Rita Herron*
wherever Harlequin Intrigue books
and ebooks are sold!

Read on for a sneak peek of
LONE RIDER
The next installment in
THE MONTANA HAMILTONS *series*
from New York Times *bestselling author*
B.J. Daniels.
*When danger claims her, rescue comes from the one
man she least expects...*

CHAPTER ONE

THE MOMENT JACE CALDER saw his sister's face, he feared the worst. His heart sank. Emily, his troubled little sister, had been doing so well since she'd gotten the job at the Sarah Hamilton Foundation in Big Timber, Montana.

"What's wrong?" he asked as he removed his Stetson, pulled up a chair at the Big Timber Java coffee shop and sat down across from her. Tossing his hat on the seat of an adjacent chair, he braced himself for bad news.

Emily blinked her big blue eyes. Even though she was closing in on twenty-five, he often caught glimpses of the girl she'd been. Her pixie cut, once a dark brown like his own hair, was dyed black. From thirteen on, she'd been piercing anything she could. At sixteen she'd begun getting tattoos and drinking. It wasn't until she'd turned seventeen that she'd run away, taken up with a thirty-year-old biker drug-dealer thief and ended up in jail for the first time.

But while Emily still had the tattoos and the piercings, she'd changed after the birth of her daughter, and after snagging this job with Bo Hamilton.

"What's wrong is Bo," his sister said. Bo had insisted her employees at the foundation call her by her first name. "Pretty cool for a boss, huh?" his sister had said at the time. He'd been surprised. That didn't sound like the woman he knew.

But who knew what was in Bo's head lately. Four months ago her mother, Sarah, who everyone believed dead the past twenty-two years, had suddenly shown up out of nowhere. According to what he'd read in the papers, Sarah had no memory of the past twenty-two years.

He'd been worried it would hurt the foundation named for her. Not to mention what a shock it must have been for Bo.

Emily leaned toward him and whispered, "Bo's… She's gone."

"Gone?"

"Before she left Friday, she told me that she would be back by ten this morning. She hasn't shown up, and no one knows where she is."

That *did* sound like the Bo Hamilton he knew. The thought of her kicked up that old ache inside him. He'd been glad when Emily had found a job and moved back to town with her baby girl. But he'd often wished her employer had been anyone but Bo Hamilton—the woman he'd once asked to marry him.

He'd spent the past five years avoiding Bo, which wasn't easy in a county as small as Sweet Grass. Crossing paths with her, even after five years, still hurt. It riled him in a way that only made him mad at himself for letting her get to him after all this time.

"What do you mean, *gone*?" he asked now.

Emily looked pained. "I probably shouldn't be telling you this—"

"Em," he said impatiently. She'd been doing so well at this job, and she'd really turned her life around. He couldn't bear the thought that Bo's disappearance might derail her second chance. Em's three-year-old daughter Jodie desperately needed her mom to stay on track.

Leaning closer again, she whispered, "Apparently there are funds missing from the foundation. An auditor's been going over all the records since Friday."

He sat back in surprise. No matter what he thought of

Bo, he'd never imagined this. The woman was already rich. She wouldn't need to divert funds…

"And that's not the worst of it," Emily said. "I was told she's on a camping trip in the mountains."

"So, she isn't really gone."

Em waved a hand. "She took her camping gear, saddled up and left Saturday afternoon. Apparently she's the one who called the auditor, so she knew he would be finished and wanting to talk to her this morning!"

Jace considered this news. If Bo really were on the run with the money, wouldn't she take her passport and her SUV as far as the nearest airport? But why would she run at all? He doubted Bo had ever had a problem that her daddy, the senator, hadn't fixed for her. She'd always had a safety net. Unlike him.

He'd been on his own since eighteen. He'd been a senior in high school, struggling to pay the bills, hang on to the ranch and raise his wild kid sister after his parents had been killed in a small plane crash. He'd managed to save the ranch, but he hadn't been equipped to raise Emily and had made his share of mistakes.

A few months ago, his sister had gotten out of jail and gone to work for Bo. He'd been surprised she'd given Emily a chance. He'd had to readjust his opinion of Bo—but only a little. Now this.

"There has to be an explanation," he said, even though he knew firsthand that Bo often acted impulsively. She did whatever she wanted, damn the world. But now his little sister was part of that world. How could she leave Emily and the rest of the staff at the foundation to face this alone?

"I sure hope everything is all right," his sister said. "Bo is so sweet."

Sweet wasn't a word he would have used to describe her. Sexy in a cowgirl way, yes, since most of the time she dressed in jeans, boots and a Western shirt—all of which accented her very nice curves. Her long, sandy-blond hair was often pulled up in a ponytail or wrestled into a braid that hung over one shoulder. Since her wide green eyes didn't need makeup to give her that girl-next-door look, she seldom wore it.

"I can't believe she wouldn't show up. Something must have happened," Emily said loyally.

He couldn't help being skeptical based on Bo's history. But given Em's concern, he didn't want to add his own kindling to the fire.

"Jace, I just have this bad feeling. You're the best tracker in these parts. I know it's a lot to ask, but would you go find her?"

He almost laughed. Given the bad blood between him and Bo? "I'm the last person—"

"I'm really worried about her. I know she wouldn't run off."

Jace wished *he* knew that. "Look, if you're really that concerned, maybe you should call the sheriff. He can get search and rescue—"

"No," Emily cried. "No one knows what's going on over at the foundation. We have to keep this quiet. That's why you have to go."

He'd never been able to deny his little sister anything, but this was asking too much.

"Please, Jace."

He swore silently. Maybe he'd get lucky and Bo would return before he even got saddled up. "If you're that worried…" He got to his feet and reached for his hat, telling himself it shouldn't take him long to find Bo if she'd gone up into the Crazies, as the Crazy Mountains were known locally. He'd grown up in those mountains. His father had been an avid hunter who'd taught him everything about mountain survival.

If Bo had gone rogue with the foundation's funds…

He hated to think what that would do not only to Emily's job but also to her recovery. She idolized her boss. So did Josie, who was allowed the run of the foundation office.

But finding Bo was one thing. Bringing her back to face the music might be another. He started to say as much to Emily, but she cut him off.

"Oh, Jace, thank you so much. If anyone can find her, it's you."

He smiled at his sister as he set his Stetson firmly on his head and made her a promise. "I'll find Bo Hamilton and bring her back." One way or the other.

CHAPTER TWO

Bo Hamilton rose with the sun, packed up camp and saddled up as a squirrel chattered at her from a nearby pine tree. Overhead, high in the Crazy Mountains, Montana's big, cloudless early summer sky had turned a brilliant blue. The day was already warm. Before she'd left, she'd heard a storm was coming in, but she'd known she'd be out of the mountains long before it hit.

She'd had a devil of a time getting to sleep last night, and after tossing and turning for hours in her sleeping bag, she had finally fallen into a death-like sleep.

But this morning, she'd awakened ready to face whatever would be awaiting her tomorrow back at the office in town. Coming up here in the mountains had been the best thing she could have done. For months she'd been worried and confused as small amounts of money kept disappearing from the foundation.

Then last week, she'd realized that more than a hundred thousand dollars was gone. She'd been so shocked that she hadn't been able to breathe, let alone think. That's when she'd called in an independent auditor. She just hoped she could find out what had happened to the money before anyone got wind of it—especially her father, Senator Buckmaster Hamilton.

Her stomach roiled at the thought. He'd always been

so proud of her for taking over the reins of the foundation that bore her mother's name. All her father needed was another scandal. He was running for the presidency of the United States, something he'd dreamed of for years. Now his daughter was about to go to jail for embezzlement. She could only imagine his disappointment in her—not to mention what it might do to the foundation.

She loved the work the foundation did, helping small businesses in their community. Her father had been worried that she couldn't handle the responsibility. She'd been determined to show him he was wrong. And show herself as well. She'd grown up a lot in the past five years, and running the foundation had given her a sense of purpose she'd badly needed.

That's why she was anxious to find out the results of the audit now that her head was clear. The mountains always did that for her. Breathing in the fresh air now, she swung up in the saddle, spurred her horse and headed down the trail toward the ranch. She'd camped only a couple of hours back into the mountain, so she still had plenty of time, she thought as she rode. The last thing she wanted was to be late to meet with the auditor.

She'd known for some time that there were... *discrepancies* in foundation funds. A part of her had hoped that it was merely a mistake—that someone would realize he or she had made an error—so she wouldn't have to confront anyone about the slip.

Bo knew how naive that was, but she couldn't bear to think that one of her employees was behind the theft. Yes, her employees were a ragtag bunch. There was Albert Drum, a seventy-two-year-young former banker who worked with the recipients of the foundation loans. Emily Calder, twenty-four, took care of the website, research, communication and marketing. The only other employee was forty-eight-year-old widow Norma Branstetter, who was in charge of fund-raising.

Employees and board members reviewed the applications that came in for financial help. But Bo was the one responsible for the money that came and went through the foundation.

Unfortunately, she trusted her employees so much that she often let them run the place, including dealing with the financial end of things. She hadn't been paying close enough attention. How else could there be unexplained expenditures?

Her father had warned her about the people she hired, saying she had to be careful. But she loved giving jobs to those who desperately needed another chance. Her employees had become a second family to her.

Just the thought that one of her employees might be responsible made her sick to her stomach. True, she was a sucker for a hard-luck story. But she trusted the people she'd hired. The thought brought tears to her eyes. They all tried so hard and were so appreciative of their jobs. She refused to believe any one of them would steal from the foundation.

So what had happened to the missing funds?

She hadn't ridden far when her horse nickered and raised his head as if sniffing the wind. Spurring him forward, she continued through the dense trees. The pine boughs sighed in the breeze, releasing the smells of early summer in the mountains she'd grown up with. She loved the Crazy Mountains. She loved them especially at this time of year. They rose from the valley into high snow-capped peaks, the awe-inspiring range running for miles to the north like a mountainous island in a sea of grassy plains.

What she appreciated most about the Crazies was that a person could get lost in them, she thought. A hunter had done just that last year.

She'd ridden down the ridge some distance, the sun moving across the sky over her head, before she caught the strong smell of smoke. This morning she'd put her campfire out using the creek water nearby. Too much of Montana burned every summer because of lightning storms and careless people, so she'd made sure her fire was extinguished before she'd left.

Now reining in, she spotted the source of the smoke. A small campfire burned below her in the dense trees of a protected gully. She stared down into the camp as smoke curled up. While it wasn't that unusual to stumble across a backpacker this deep in the Crazies, it *was* strange for a camp to be so far off the trail. Also, she didn't see anyone below her on the mountain near the fire. Had whoever camped there failed to put out the fire before leaving?

Bo hesitated, feeling torn because she didn't want to take the time to ride all the way down the mountain to the out-of-the-way camp. Nor did she want to ride into anyone's camp unless necessary.

But if the camper had failed to put out the fire, that was another story.

"Hello?" she called down the mountainside.

A hawk let out a cry overhead, momentarily startling her.

"Hello?" she called again, louder.

No answer. No sign of anyone in the camp.

Bo let out an aggravated sigh and spurred her horse. She had a long ride back and didn't need a detour. But she still had plenty of time if she hurried. As she made her way down into the ravine, she caught glimpses of the camp and the smoking campfire, but nothing else.

The hidden-away camp finally came into view below her. She could see that whoever had camped there hadn't made any effort at all to put out the fire. She looked for horseshoe tracks but saw only boot prints in the dust that led down to the camp.

A quiet seemed to fall over the mountainside. No hawk called out again from high above the trees. No squirrel chattered at her from a pine bough. Even the breeze seemed to have gone silent.

Bo felt a sudden chill as if the sun had gone down—an instant before the man appeared so suddenly from out of the dense darkness of the trees. He grabbed her, yanked her down from the saddle and clamped an arm around her as he shoved the dirty blade of a knife in her face.

"Well, look at you," he said hoarsely against her ear. "Ain't you a sight for sore eyes? Guess it's my lucky day."

JACE HAD JUST knocked at the door when another truck drove up from the direction of the corrals. As Senator Buckmaster Hamilton himself opened the door, he was looking past Jace's shoulder. Jace glanced back to see Cooper Barnett climb out of his truck and walk toward them.

Jace turned back around. "I'm Jace Calder," he said, holding out his hand as the senator's gaze shifted to him.

The senator frowned but shook his hand. "I know who you are. I'm just wondering what's got you on my doorstep so early in the morning."

"I'm here about your daughter Bo."

Buckmaster looked to Cooper. "Tell me you aren't here about my daughter Olivia."

Cooper laughed. "My pregnant bride is just fine, thanks."

The senator let out an exaggerated breath and turned his attention back to Jace. "What's this about—?" But before he could finish, a tall, elegant blonde woman appeared at his side. Jace recognized Angelina Broadwater Hamilton, the senator's second wife. The rumors about her being kicked out of the house to make way for Buckmaster's first wife weren't true, it seemed.

She put a hand on Buckmaster's arm. "It's the auditor calling from the foundation office. He's looking for Bo. She didn't show up for work today, and there seems to be a problem."

"That's why I'm here," Jace said.

"Me too," Cooper said, sounding surprised.

"Come in, then," Buckmaster said, waving both men inside. Once he'd closed the big door behind them, he asked, "Now what's this about Bo?"

"I was just talking to one of the wranglers," Cooper said, jumping in ahead of Jace. "Bo apparently left Saturday afternoon on horseback, saying she'd be back this morning, but she hasn't returned."

"That's what I heard as well," Jace said, taking the opening. "I need to know where she might have gone."

Both Buckmaster and Cooper looked to him. "You sound as if you're planning to go after her," the senator said.

"I am."

"Why would you do that? I didn't think you two were seeing each other?" Cooper asked like the protective brother-in-law he was.

"We're not," Jace said.

"Wait a minute," the senator said. "You're the one who stood her up for the senior prom. I'll never forget it. My baby cried for weeks."

Jace nodded. "That would be me."

"But you've dated Bo more recently than senior prom," Buckmaster was saying.

"Five years ago," he said. "But that doesn't have anything to do with this. I have my reasons for wanting to see Bo come back. My sister works at the foundation."

"Why wouldn't Bo come back?" the senator demanded.

Behind him, Angelina made a disparaging sound. "Because there's money missing from the foundation along with your daughter." She looked at Jace. "You said your sister works down there?"

He smiled, seeing that she was clearly judgmental of the "kind of people" Bo had hired to work at the foundation. "My sister doesn't have access to any of the money, if that's what you're worried about." He turned to the senator again. "The auditor is down at the foundation office, trying to sort it out. Bo needs to be there. I thought you might have some idea where she might have gone in the mountains. I thought I'd go find her."

The senator looked to his son-in-law. Cooper shrugged.

"Cooper, you were told she planned to be back Sunday?" her father said. "She probably changed her mind or went too far, not realizing how long it would take her to get back. If she had an appointment today with an auditor, I'm sure she's on her way as we speak."

"Or she's hiding up there and doesn't want to be found," Angelina quipped from the couch. "If she took that money, she could be miles from here by now." She groaned. "It's always something with your girls, isn't it?"

"I highly doubt Bo has taken off with any foundation money," the senator said and shot his wife a disgruntled look. "Every minor problem isn't a major scandal," he said and sighed, clearly irritated with his wife.

When he and Bo had dated, she'd told him that her stepmother was always quick to blame her and her sisters no matter the situation. As far as Jace could tell, there was no love lost on either side.

"Maybe we should call the sheriff," Cooper said.

Angelina let out a cry. "That's all we need—more negative publicity. It will be bad enough when this gets out. But if search and rescue is called in and the sheriff has to go up there... For all we know, Bo could be meeting someone in those mountains."

Jace hadn't considered she might have an accomplice. "That's why I'm the best person to go after her."

"How do you figure that?" Cooper demanded, giving him a hard look.

"She already doesn't like me, and the feeling is mutual. Maybe you're right and she's hightailing it home as we speak," Jace said. "But whatever's going on with her, I'm going to find her and make sure she gets back."

"You sound pretty confident of that," the senator said sounding almost amused.

"I know these mountains, and I'm not a bad tracker. I'll find her. But that's big country. My search would go faster if I have some idea where she was headed when she left."

"There's a trail to the west of the ranch that connects with the Sweet Grass Creek trail," her father said.

Jace rubbed a hand over his jaw. "That trail forks not far up."

"She usually goes to the first camping spot before the fork," the senator said. "It's only a couple of hours back in. I'm sure she wouldn't go any farther than that. It's along Loco Creek."

"I know that spot," Jace said.

Cooper looked to his father-in-law. "You want me to get some men together and go search for her? That makes more sense than sending—"

Buckmaster shook his head and turned to Jace. "I remember your father. The two of you were volunteers on a search years ago. I was impressed with both of you. I'm putting my money on you finding her if she doesn't turn up on her own. I'll give you 'til sundown."

"Make it twenty-four hours. There's a storm coming so I plan to be back before it hits. If we're both not back by then, send in the cavalry," he said and with a tip of his hat, headed for the door.

Behind him, he heard Cooper say, "Sending him could be a mistake."

"The cowboy's mistake," Buckmaster said. "I know my daughter. She's on her way back, and she isn't going to like that young man tracking her down. Jace Calder is the one she almost married."

* * * * *

Find out what happens next in
LONE RIDER
by New York Times
bestselling author B.J. Daniels
available August 2015,
wherever HQN Books and ebooks are sold.
www.Harlequin.com

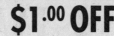

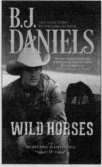
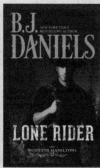
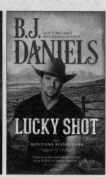